S0-EWH-272

Dan Carter and the Cub Honor

The Cubs spent every spare hour
in the church gymnasium *(See page 70)*
Dan Carter and the Cub Honor

DAN CARTER

and the
CUB HONOR

by

Mildred A. Wirt

ILLUSTRATED

CUPPLES AND LEON COMPANY
Publishers   *New York*

Copyright, 1953, by
CUPPLES AND LEON COMPANY

ALL RIGHTS RESERVED

Dan Carter and the Cub Honor

Printed in the United States of America

CONTENTS

Chapter		Page
1.	A New Cub	1
2.	In Quest of a Freezer	15
3.	A Tapping Bell	26
4.	Payment Refused	35
5.	A Threatening Suit	44
6.	A Challenge from Pat	52
7.	"Know Your Neighborhood"	65
8.	A Wish Fulfilled	77
9.	Strawberry Ice Cream	86
10.	Old Terry's Demand	102
11.	The Locked Door	112
12.	Rules of Basketball	121
13.	Halloween Pranks	131
14.	The Belfry Bell	143
15.	Measles	149
16.	The Stranger	160
17.	A Witness	169
18.	A Jolt for Pat	179
19.	Cub Honor	189
20.	Proof	205

CHAPTER 1

A NEW CUB

SKILLFULLY, Dan Carter dribbled the basketball down the polished gymnasium floor. With an easy toss of his right hand, he looped it neatly through the basket.

"Nice going, Dan," approved Brad Wilber, the Den Chief, who directed the Cub Scout practice.

The five boys, all members of Den 2, were practicing in the basement of First Methodist Church. Now after a brisk half-hour work-out, they were ready to adjourn to the upstairs clubroom for their weekly business session.

Dan tossed the ball to Midge Holloway, who passed it to Red Suell. The latter shot a fast one to Chips Davis, who fumbled. He awkwardly recovered the ball, but in attempting a basket, missed it by several inches.

"Butter fingers; Butter fingers!" mocked a voice from the basement window.

The Cubs had not realized that they were being

watched. Turning quickly toward the wall behind them, they saw several boyish and jeering faces pressed against the rain-streaked panes.

"It's Pat Oswald and his gang," Brad instantly recognized them. "Don't pay any attention."

Acting on the Den Chief's suggestion, the Cubs tried to ignore the boys at the window. But it was quite impossible.

Nervous because he knew he was being watched, Dan tried a long shot from mid-floor, and missed the basket. Again Pat and his followers hooted.

"Look at 'im!" one of the tormentors yelled. "Why, even a girl could do better than that!"

Dan could not endure the taunt. He walked over to the window.

"Oh, yeah?" he demanded. "I suppose you're so good you never miss!"

"Dead-eye Pat, that's me name!" the older boy boasted. "Come on, guys, let's show 'em!"

Boldly, he pushed open the window which swung on hinges. Before the Cubs could stop him, Pat shoved his muscular torso through the opening, and leaped down onto the gymnasium floor. Behind him, like so many spry grasshoppers, came three of his cronies. The boys ranged in age from 7 to 11

A New Cub

years, but all were gangling and over-sized.

"Hey, you!" Red Suell cried furiously. "Get out of here! You got no business coming in!"

"Yah, yah, yah!" mocked Pat. He gave Red a hard shove, deliberately tearing the basketball from his grasp.

"Come on, fellows!" he urged his gang. "Let's show these babies how to play ball!"

He dribbled in beneath the basket. Without appearing to take aim, he carelessly hooked the ball up toward the netting. Neatly, it swished through.

Despite their annoyance, the Cubs were impressed. Pat was plenty good! No argument about that. His flashy skill so amazed them that they did not try to recover the ball.

One of the invaders snatched and passed it back to Pat. From that moment, it became a teasing, tormenting game of "keep it away from the Cubs."

"You've no right to come in here and break up our practice." Chips Davis accused hotly. "Give me that ball!"

He rushed in to snatch it. Pat with jeering laughter, passed it on to another boy in his group.

"Give us our ball!" Chips shouted again. "If you don't hand it over—"

"Yah, yah, yah," mocked Pat. "Here it is, baby!"

He heaved the ball with terrific force. It struck the surprised Chips in the pit of his stomach, doubling him over.

At this moment, Sam Hatfield, the Cubmaster, appeared in the gymnasium doorway. The athletic coach and leader in the citywide Pack had a knack of getting on well with all types of boys. Now, as if he had noted nothing amiss, he commented cheerfully:

"Well, well, I see we have some new recruits today."

"Recruits, nothing!" snorted Midge Holloway. "These hoodlums are trying to take over the gym—that's what!"

"Aw, we were only having a little fun," Pat growled. Already he was edging toward the door. "Come on, fellows. Let's scram!"

As quickly as they had come, the intruders were gone. Mr. Hatfield waited until the door had slammed behind them, and then asked Brad about the youngsters.

"That was Pat Oswald and his bunch from out Bay Shore Road way," the Den Chief replied. "They're always making trouble."

A New Cub

The Cubmaster offered no comment except to remind the Cubs that it was time for the meeting to start.

"Where's Fred?" Dan asked, noticing that Mr. Hatfield's son was not with him.

"He's waiting upstairs in the meeting room," Mr. Hatfield replied. "He's getting acquainted with our new Den member."

"New member?" Dan asked quickly. The other Cubs, hearing the remark, gathered about to ask questions. This was the first hint they'd had that a new boy had joined the group.

"Come along and meet him," Mr. Hatfield invited.

Chips, Red and Midge rushed on ahead up the stone stairway. Deliberately, the Cub leader lingered behind to speak privately to Brad and Dan.

"As a special favor to me, I wish you fellows would look after Chub," he said quietly. "Teach him the ropes."

"Chub?" Dan questioned. "The new Cub?"

"Yes, his name is Charles Weldon." Mr. Hatfield hesitated slightly before he spoke the boy's surname. Then he went on "He's a shy youngster, not very sure of himself yet. Don't tease him about his family background. Don't ask questions, and don't let the others do it either."

5

Brad and Dan were astonished by the request for usually Mr. Hatfield held to the theory that every Cub should fend for himself. Who was Chub, they wondered? Why had he never attended their school?

"Chub is new in Webster City," Mr. Hatfield said, as if picking the question from their minds. "Not much is known about his parents. He lives with Mrs. Lornsdale at the west edge of town."

"Is he an orphan?" Dan inquired.

"Something like that," Mr. Hatfield purposely was vague as he locked the basketball into an equipment case. "Now I've told you all anyone needs to know about Chub. No more questions. Pass the word along that no one is to tease him."

"Sure," Dan agreed. "Brad and I will look out for him."

Their curiosity heightened by the information Mr. Hatfield had given them, the two boys scarcely could wait to meet the new Cub.

Brad and Dan both were "veterans" of the organization and Mr. Hatfield depended upon them a great deal. Brad was a serious, dark-haired youngster of 13, and the only Boy Scout in the organization. Even-tempered always, he had a quiet but efficient way of getting things done.

A New Cub

Though younger, Dan likewise was efficient and highly reliable. A fine athlete for his years, he also was quick in school and his original ideas helped make the den a success. He had been chosen denner because of his popularity.

Upstairs, the boys found Fred Hatfield waiting with Chub.

Pouring into the cheerful club room, the Cubs cast covert glances at the new boy.

Chub was 10, short and stubby, with a crop of chocolate brown freckles. A thatch of yellow, curly hair hung down almost to the bridge of his pug nose. He did not have the blue Cub uniform, but wore a suit with sleeves a trifle too short.

As Mr. Hatfield introduced the Cubs one by one, Chub smiled shyly and stammered a few words. The leader then started the meeting off with roll call and a peppy song to the tune of "America."

"Cub friendships, pure and deep,
We promise we will keep
Our pledge to thee;
We will honor and obey Akela all the way
And on that twelfth birthday
Good Scouts we'll be!"

For Chub's benefit, Mr. Hatfield then explained that to qualify as a Bobcat he must learn the Cub Promise and to repeat the Law of the Pack. Other requirements were that he understand the meaning of WEBELOS, and know how to give the Cub sign and handshake, the Cub motto and the salute.

A Bobcat, the leader further explained, signified the first step in Cubbing. Other progressive ranks were Wolf, Bear and Lion.

"A Cub always does his part," he emphasized. "Above all, honor is his most sacred possession."

By this time Chub had begun to look worried. To relieve his mind, Mr. Hatfield assured him that it would not take long to learn all the essentials.

"The other Cubs will help you," he promised.

"Sure we will," said Dan, picking up his cue.

Mr. Hatfield went on to say that the theme of the Pack for that month would be to "Know your Neighborhood." Each den, he told the group, would be given opportunity to visit interesting places in the community.

At this point the talk was interrupted by a slight scratching noise at one of the windows. The Cubs, twisting in their chairs, again saw grinning faces pressed against the glass panes.

A New Cub

"Pat and his gang!" Red Suell exploded. "Those pests have been listening!"

"Lets drive 'em away!" proposed Midge, jumping up from his chair.

"Why not invite them inside?" countered Mr. Hatfield. With a smile, he started toward the window.

However, the Bay Shore boys, observing the Cubmaster's approach, ducked back out of sight. With a shrug, Mr. Hatfield resumed the meeting. He told the Cubs more about the Know Your Community visits which were being planned, and asked for suggested trips.

"How about one to the fire station?" piped up Chips eagerly. "Maybe they'd let us ride the engine on a trial run."

"I'd like to visit a newspaper office." This proposal came from Midge, whose father, Burton Holloway, was an active Den Dad.

"The courthouse!" suggested Dan. "It would be interesting to watch a trial."

Other ideas came thick and fast. In fact, with the exception of Chub, every boy immediately thought of at least one place suitable for a Den visit.

"Chub doesn't know Webster City well, because

he hasn't lived here long," Mr. Hatfield remarked. "He'll think of a place before our next meeting. His suggestion may be the best of all."

"That's right," agreed Dan. "All the places we've hit on so far are the obvious ones. Probably every Den in Webster City will come up with the same ones. I wish we could think of an out-of-the-way place to visit."

"Chub will ring the bell," predicted Brad. "Are we to visit all the places, Mr. Hatfield?"

"Only the most interesting. After all the suggestions are in, we'll vote on it. Now, one more matter. About that party we're giving for the parents a week from Friday night. Shall we serve real homemade ice cream?"

"Swell," approved Midge, smacking his lips. "Chocolate with nuts in it!"

"The mothers have promised to furnish the cake," Mr. Hatfield resumed. "Angel food, spice and chocolate. Making the ice cream will be our job. Know where we can get a couple of old-fashioned ice cream freezers?"

"My grandmother had one, but I think she gave it away," Dan said doubtfully.

A New Cub

"Large freezers may not be easy to find. Well, see what you can do about it, boys, and report back."

The afternoon meeting broke up quickly for the hour was late. As the Cubs poured out of the clubroom, Dan brushed against Pat Oswald who had been standing close to the wall.

"Listening again!" he said scornfully. "If you want to learn about Cub Scouts, why don't you come inside instead of sneaking around like a cat?"

"You're calling me an alley cat?" Pat demanded. He doubled up his fists and glared at Dan. "Say, I ought to knock the stuffins out of you!"

"Want to try?"

"Cut it," Brad advised quietly. "We're not getting into a fight here in the churchyard. Or anywhere else for that matter."

"Naw, the Cubs wouldn't fight," Pat jeered. "They're yellow. Afraid of their sissy shadows."

"That's not true!"

"Can't even hang onto a basketball," Pat went on with his tormenting. "Sissies!"

"And look at that little panty-waist with curls!" shouted one of the boys in Pat's gang. He had singled Chub out for attention.

Walking over to the shy boy, he gave his corduroy suit jacket a hard jerk. Chub cringed back into the doorway.

"Scared, ain't you?"

"You leave Chub alone," Dan said, stepping in front of the new Cub member.

The other boy fell back a step, but not because of Dan's command. In truth, he had caught a glimpse of Mr. Hatfield coming down the corridor to the church doorway.

"What goes on here?" the Cub leader demanded, and this time his voice was stern.

With shouts of laughter, Pat and his followers ran off down the street, rattling a string of tin cans.

"That Pat is a mean one," Chips declared. "He'd have started trouble if you hadn't come along, Mr. Hatfield."

"Possibly," conceded the Cub leader. "Pat is inclined to be a bully, but he's mostly bluff, I think. My guess is that he and his pals really are envious of the good times the Cubs have here."

"Especially of our basketball practice," added Brad.

Mr. Hatfield advised the Cubs not to take Pat's teasing too seriously.

A New Cub

"Who knows?" he suggested as the group broke up. "If you work at the job, the Bay Shore boys may be won over as friends. That would be much better than having them as enemies."

The Cubs were far from certain that they wanted the Bay Shore boys as friends. However, they kept their thoughts to themselves.

As the Cubs started home, Dan fell into step with Brad. During the brisk walk, the younger boy had little to say. Finally, Brad commented upon his unusual silence.

"Worrying about where we can get a couple of ice cream freezers, Dan?"

"Not exactly. I'll admit I was thinking about the party though."

"Something seems to be bothering you."

"I was wondering about Pat. He and his gang were listening at the church door when we made plans for the social a week from Friday."

"Probably."

"I'm sure of it," Dan insisted soberly. "This is what worries me. I'm afraid Pat and his bunch may show up at the party and really stir up a mess."

Brad glanced down at the younger boy, surprised by the intensity of his remark.

"Sort of borrowing trouble, aren't you, Dan?"

"I guess so," Dan admitted with a rueful laugh. "But Pat's a sly one. I sure hope I'm wrong, but I'm terribly afraid he intends to try to break up our Den."

CHAPTER 2

IN QUEST OF A FREEZER

THE Carter kitchen was fragrant with the odor of frying bacon as Dan bounced down the stairs next morning for an eight o'clock breakfast. It was Saturday and a beautiful crisp October day. Dan had plans for every hour ahead.

"Mom," he began, sliding into his usual chair at the foot of the breakfast table. "Do you know where I can get an ice cream freezer?"

Dan's odd requests long since had ceased to astonish Mrs. Carter. "You mean the old fashioned kind one turns with a crank?" she asked, pouring orange juice into tall glasses.

"We need a couple of large ones," Dan explained. "Our Den is throwing a big party for the Mothers and Dads. No freezer—no party."

"My mother had one, but that was long ago. Let me think—oh, I recall the old Christian Church on River Road had several large ones."

"Think I could borrow 'em, Mom?"

"That depends, Dan. The old church was abandoned about a year ago. When last I heard, the freezers and other kitchen equipment were stored in the basement. I doubt any of them were moved to the new church building."

Now that his mother mentioned it, Dan recalled that the Christian Church had been boarded up nearly a year. The building had been offered for sale, but so far no buyer had showed interest. Meanwhile, the place was supervised by Terry Treuhaft, an elderly caretaker, who had his own little cottage not far from the river.

"You might talk to Mr. Treuhaft about it," Mrs. Carter remarked. "If the freezers are still there, I see no reason why the Cubs shouldn't have them for the party."

"I'll round up some of the Cubs and hike out to his cottage," Dan decided. He buttered a second slice of toast and scooped the last piece of bacon from the platter. "How's chances for a pack lunch, Mom?"

"Fairly good, I guess," his mother smiled. "That is, providing you rake the yard first. The leaves have been falling fast."

In Quest of a Freezer

"Oh, Mom! That will take an age. How about doing it when I get back?"

"A Cub in hand is worth two on a hike, Dan. Once you get away on such a lovely day as this, I know I'll never see you again until nightfall. Work before fun, you know."

"Okay," Dan gave in with a grin. "I'll get right at it. First, though, I want to call some of the Cubs to ask them to hike with me to the old church."

"Don't forget to invite the new boy," his mother reminded him. "Charles Weldon—is that his name?"

"We call him Chub. He's a queer one, Mom. Shy as a mouse. I don't know if he'd like to hike—"

"At any rate, be sure to invite him," Mrs. Carter urged.

Dan felt a bit ashamed of not wanting Chub. It wasn't that he had anything against the new Cub. But somehow, he didn't feel as well acquainted with him as he did with Chips, Midge, Red, Brad or Fred.

To please his mother, he called Chub's home first of all. The phone was answered by Mrs. Lornsdale, the widow, with whom the boy lived.

Charles was there, she said, and she was certain

he would want to join the group of Cubs. She promised to have him meet the boys at the old church.

In rapid succession, Dan then called all the others except Mack Tibbets who was out of town for two weeks. To his disappointment, Brad Wilber could not go, having work to do at home. Chips, Red and Midge eagerly accepted the invitation.

"Come over to my house as soon as your lunch is packed," Dan requested. "I have to rake leaves, but I'll be through before you can snap your bubble gum!"

By eleven o'clock, a huge pile of leaves at the curb attested to the furious pace of Dan's labors. Nevertheless, a third of the yard remained unraked when Midge and Chips arrived with knapsacks slung over their shoulders.

"Want to help?" Dan suggested hopefully. "I got an extra rake."

The two Cubs took turns and soon the work was practically finished.

"Where's Red?" Dan demanded.

Just then he glimpsed the red-headed youngster coming down the walk dribbling a basketball.

"Hey, where'd you get that?" Midge asked with keen interest as the boy joined the group.

In Quest of a Freezer

"Bought it with my paper money. Here, catch!"

Red made a fast pass, and Midge, not expecting the ball, missed it.

"Gee, you're awkward," Red teased. "If you don't improve, we'll have to get another forward on our Cub team."

"Over my dead body!" Recovering the ball, Midge threw it hard at Red, who also missed.

"It looks to me as if we all need more practice in passing," Dan remarked as he put away the rakes. "Taking the ball with you on the hike, Red?"

"Sure. Why not?"

"Maybe we'll get a chance to practice a bit after lunch. Bring it along, Red."

The boys started off for Terry Treuhaft's cottage, only a block from the old Christian Church. Enjoying the soft, balmy air, they scuffed along a river path, between tall trees which rapidly were shedding their bright-hued leaves.

"Swell day for a roast," Chips said, blinking in the bright sun. "I wish we'd brought some weiners."

The boys presently came within view of Terry Treuhaft's white clapboard cottage. The church caretaker, a bent old man with gnarled hands, was building a fence in the back yard. He scarcely glanced up as the boys halted beside him.

Finally as the hammering went on and on, Dan introduced himself and explained the purpose of the call. He told of the organization's need of ice cream freezers.

"What's that?" Mr. Treuhaft asked gruffly. "Ice cream at this time of year? Stuff and nonsense! Fiddle Faddle! Why tell me about it anyhow?"

"The Christian Church has some freezers in the basement," Chips interposed. "Aren't you the caretaker?"

"So that's the angle?" Old Terry hammered a nail which went crooked into the board. He uttered an enraged exclamation. "Drat it! Can't you boys see you're bothering me? I'm busy as all get-out. I want to finish this fence before sun down."

"We do need the freezers," Dan persisted. "Couldn't you let us have them?"

"I'm busy," Old Terry repeated between loud bangs of his hammer. "Busy! I've no time to go over to the church now. Come back Monday or later in the week and we'll talk about it."

"How about letting us have the key ourselves?" proposed Red. "We could get the freezers and return it."

In Quest of a Freezer

"No one gets that key," Old Terry said with emphasis. "The trustees hold me responsible for everything that is stored in the church. I'm taking no chances on a bunch of kids."

"We wouldn't touch anything," Red insisted, but the caretaker cut him short.

"Move along, boys," he said crossly. "I said come back next week."

Thus dismissed, the Cubs trudged off, deeply discouraged. Not even Dan had an idea where another freezer could be obtained. Old Terry's attitude annoyed the boys, for in Webster City the Den 2 Cubs had earned a reputation for dependability.

On one occasion, the boys had by their quick and efficient work, saved a pheasant raiser from losing his most valuable birds in a flash flood. Even more recently, they had enjoyed adventure in solving a mystery. This story of their encounter with Indians, has been told in the volume entitled, "Dan Carter and the Great Carved Face."

"We may as well eat our lunch somewhere along the river, and then go home," Midge proposed glumly. "It's long past noon."

"I'm hungry too," Chips added. "Let's eat."

"First, we have to go to the church," Dan said. "I invited Chub to have lunch with us. He's been waiting there an age now."

A little silence greeted Dan's announcement. But the Cubs were too well trained in sportsmanship to make pointed remarks about the new Den member. Their very silence, though, told Dan that they weren't too happy about including him in the outing.

"Let's move along then," Red said impatiently. "The quicker we find Chub, the quicker we eat."

A little farther on, the Cubs came within view of the old weatherbeaten Christian Church. The lawn, once a velvety green, now was overgrown with weeds. They were especially high in the old cemetery on the slope leading down to the river.

The church building itself was in need of paint. Roof shingles curled with age, and a tower bell had reddened with rust.

"I don't see Chub anywhere around here," Chips declared, looking around the grounds.

"Maybe he's around back," Dan said. He shouted Chub's name several times.

Almost at once the Cubs heard pounding footsteps. Chub came running around the corner of the old church, his hair rumpled by the wind.

In Quest of a Freezer

"Gee, I'm glad you finally came," he cried, stammering in his eagerness. "It was sort of scarey waiting here so long."

"Scarey?" Red demanded. "What is there to be afraid of?"

"The old graveyard does have a spooky look," Dan said quickly before Chub could answer.

"It doesn't scare me," Red boasted. "I wouldn't be afraid to come here alone at night either, I bet."

"Want to try it?" Chips caught him up.

Red let the challenge pass. The boys found a grassy site at the rear of the building and spread out their sandwiches.

Dan discovered that his Mother had packed extra fruit and cookies, so he shared them with Chub who had brought only a peanut butter sandwich and an apple.

Red, a fast eater, finished ahead of the others and restlessly began to wander about. Soon he was peering into the dusty basement windows of the church.

"What do you see?" Dan inquired curiously.

"Not much of anything cept an old furnace."

"Any sign of those ice cream freezers?"

"I can see some cooking junk on one of the shelves. Don't know if it's a freezer or not—"

Their interest whetted, the other boys gathered up the loose picnic papers and went to join Red. From another window on the opposite side of the building, Dan obtained a much better view of the cluttered basement interior.

"I do see a freezer!" he reported gleefully. "I'm sure of it!"

"Wow, I wish we could have it," Red declared. "If we could just get down into the basement—say, maybe we can find an unlocked window!"

"Nothing doing," Dan said with firmness. "Even if we found one, we couldn't go into the building after Old Terry told us to wait. Cub honor."

"Oh, I was only talking," Red answered with a shrug. "I didn't really intend to go inside."

Dan's window offered a fairly clear view of the church basement, so the other boys crowded about to peer down into the pillared room.

"The place has a lot of boxes," Midge observed. "Some of 'em look as if they've been smashed open. I see some tools too. A coal shovel—"

His voice broke on the last named object and an eerie silence came upon all the Cubs. Was it imagination, or had they heard a strange sound—the faint tap-tap-tap of the overhead church bell?

In Quest of a Freezer

"What was that?" Midge demanded.

"G-ghosts," mumbled Chub, his voice choked with fright. In a hushed whisper he added the plea: "Come on, f-fellows, let's get away from here q-quick!"

CHAPTER 3

A TAPPING BELL

CHUB'S squeal of fright unnerved the other Cubs for an instant. But they did not give way to panic. Chips grasped the younger boy's arm, holding him as he would have fled from the church grounds.

"Take it easy," he advised. "There aren't any ghosts and we all know it."

"I-I heard something," Chub said, half ashamed. "It sounded like a bell tapping."

The Cubs stood gazing up at the belfry. So far as they could see, the rusty old bell hung absolutely motionless.

"You imagined it," Red said gruffly. "How could that bell jingle?"

"I thought I heard it tap myself," Midge said.

"Maybe the wind moved the bell," Red offered as an explanation. "It's blowing fairly strong from the direction of the river."

The other Cubs nodded agreement, satisfied that the mystery was solved. Dan remained silent. He too had heard the metallic sound which had startled

A Tapping Bell

Chub, and has assumed it to be a tapping bell. But to theorize that the wind had been responsible, seemed silly.

Nevertheless, not caring to further alarm the Cubs, he did not reveal his thoughts.

"Come on, let's practice basketball," Red urged to break the uneasy silence which had fallen upon the group. "Here, Midge, catch!"

He tossed the ball to his friend, who passed it back. The boys spread out, palming the basketball from one to another, faster and faster. Then they played "keep away" for a few minutes. Chub was less skillful than the other Cubs, frequently letting the ball slip from his fingers.

"I don't know why I'm so awkward," he said miserably.

"You'll catch on all at once," Dan encouraged him. "Here, pass me a fast, hard one now."

Chub swung the ball in a wide arch and heaved with all his strength. His aim was distressingly bad.

The ball sailed high above Dan's reach, over the bushes and through a window.

A stunned silence came upon the Cubs as they heard the crash and beheld the damage.

"Wow! You've done it now, Chub," Chips said pityingly.

"We'll all catch it from Old Terry," Midge added, staring at the jagged hole in the pane. "I guess we'll have to pay for the damage."

"It was a-all my fault," Chub admitted, close to tears. "How much do windows cost?"

"Oh, a dollar or two," Midge said vaguely. "Maybe more."

Tears began to roll down Chub's cheeks.

"Don't let it throw you," Dan said, slapping him on the shoulders. "Breaking a window can happen to anyone."

"It's not that," Chub mumbled, his eyes downcast. "How am I going to pay? I-I don't have hardly any spending money. And I can't ask Mrs. Lornsdale to help me. I wish I'd never joined the Cubs! Then I wouldn't be in this awful mess."

"Hey, cut out that kind of talk!" Dan said. "You're not in any mess. It's not fair either, to blame the Cubs for this. It was just an accident."

"I didn't mean that about the Cubs. I'll get the money somehow."

"Forget it," Dan advised. "It was as much my fault as it was yours that the window was smashed. I told you to throw the ball hard, didn't I?"

"Yes, but—"

A Tapping Bell

"And I was standing in front of the church window, Chub. So it was more my fault than it was yours. I'll see Old Terry first thing tomorrow and settle for the window."

"Pay it all, you mean?" Midge asked in surprise.

"Sure," Dan replied. "I have some money saved. It won't strap me."

Though he spoke carelessly, the denner had struggled inwardly before making his generous offer. For weeks he had been hoarding every penny, intending to buy a basketball of his own. Now he'd have to forget about it.

"You shouldn't pay for a window I broke," Chub insisted, but he plainly was relieved by the offer. "I-I'll try to pay you back."

"Just forget it," Dan advised. "Set your mind on those tests you have to pass for Cubs. Know the Cub handclasp yet?"

Chub shook his head.

Dan showed him the grasp with the first finger extended straight along the inside of the other person's wrist.

"Tell me what WEBELOS means too," Chub said eagerly.

"The letters WBL stand for Cub ranks," Dan explained. "Wolf-Bear-Lion. 'We'll be loyal.' Get it?"

"I guess so. But what does the "S" stand for?"

"Scout. The letters WBLS form the skeleton or framework of the Indian tribal name, Webelos."

"Cubs are supposed to be cheerful, helpful and friendly always," Midge declared.

"Brave too," added Red significantly as he moved toward the bushes to retrieve the lost basketball.

Chub flushed, knowing full well that reference was being made to the jittery way he had talked about ghosts.

"I've got a lot to learn," he said soberly. "I want to be a Cub the worst way. I'll try awfully hard."

"Sure you will," Dan declared with a friendly grin. "You'll make it too. At first it seems as if there's a lot to learn. Know the Law of the Pack yet?"

"I think so. But what is the Pack?"

"Gee whiskers! You are dumb!" Red snorted, coming back with the basketball tucked under his arm.

"You're violating one of the Cub rules right now," Dan informed Red. "A Cub is supposed to be courteous."

"Aw, I didn't mean anything! I'm sorry, Chub."

A Tapping Bell

"I don't mind being called dumb, because I am. But I'm catching on a little."

The Cubs warmed to the boy, liking the way he admitted his shortcomings. He might be young, but he was eager and willing, and that was what counted.

"You asked about the Pack," Dan said, taking up Chub's question. "It's an association of Dens. Every month all the Den members have a big gathering of the citywide Pack. Believe me, those are some pow-wows!"

"Say, don't you wish the Pack would pull off a basketball tournament," remarked Red. "Wonder if Den 1 has a team?"

"We couldn't get 'em interested," Dan regretfully reported. "They're going out for swimming this fall."

"What's the use having a Cub team unless we can round up competition?"

"We'll find some," Dan promised. "First, though, we ought to get our own team better organized. We can stand a lot of practice."

"You can say that again," Chips agreed, gazing at the jagged hole in the window.

The unfortunate accident had somewhat dampened the high spirits of the Cubs. Abruptly, Red announced that it was time for him to go home. His departure also was a signal for the others to leave.

Dan walked with Chub, telling him again not to worry about the smashed glass.

"It shouldn't cost much to repair the damage," he declared. "I'll see Old Terry about it right away. No use waiting."

"I'll go with you," Chub offered. "I can't let you take all the blame."

The Treuhaft cottage had a deserted appearance as the boys approached. Old Terry had abandoned his fence building and all his tools had been put away. Though Dan pounded repeatedly on the door, there was no answer.

"He's off somewhere," Dan commented. "Oh, well, no use waiting. I'll come back here tomorrow after church."

The boys parted, Chub returning to the widow's home at the outskirts of Webster City.

Dan sauntered on alone, enjoying the nice air and thinking about the events of the day. He liked Chub and intended to look out for him. All the same,

A Tapping Bell

it struck him as odd that the boy never revealed anything about himself. Why had Mr. Hatfield requested that no questions be asked? Did he have special information about Chub that he was keeping to himself?

"I'm getting as curious as an old tabby cat," Dan chided himself. "Guess I'll have all I can do to look after my own affairs."

His way took him past the old church. Dan had no intention of stopping. Nevertheless, he did glance toward the belfry, visible through the half-naked trees.

"Queer about that tapping bell," he mused. "I know I heard it. Since it couldn't have been the wind, a bird must have flown against the clapper."

The explanation satisfied Dan for the moment, and he smiled in relief. How naive Chub had been to suggest a ghost! Not that the old decaying church didn't have an eerie appearance with its dead vines and look of utter desolation.

Bushes had overgrown nearly all of the church walls. The mass of crimson and yellow leaves against stone and brick made a pretty splash of color, Dan thought. But Old Terry really should whack down the brush a bit, even with winter coming on.

Dan's thoughts were roving, when suddenly his attention focused upon a tall, mis-shapen evergreen at the west side of the old building. He halted to stare.

The little tree was moving jerkily, as if alive.

"What the dickens?" Dan muttered.

As he watched, a shadowy figure slithered from behind the foliage and vanished toward the graveyard.

CHAPTER 4

PAYMENT REFUSED

DAN stood very still for a moment, staring fixedly at the place where the shadowy figure had disappeared. He wasn't sure what he had seen, or for that matter whether he had observed anything.

Had his approach frightened away someone who had been loitering at the rear windows of the old church? So far as he could see from the road, no one now was lurking in the cemetery. However, the tilted tombstones offered many hiding places.

Dan briefly considered ambling over to study the layout but decided against it. The hour was late and he was due home. Besides the old church stood in an isolated area, easily accessible to tramps who might come up the slope from the river area.

"No use asking for trouble," he thought. "Whoever was prowling around, probably wasn't doing any harm."

Dan waited a few minutes longer, thinking he might again glimpse the elusive figure. Seeing no one, he trudged on home.

Sunday was a pleasant, quiet day in the Carter

household. Dan attended church school in the morning as was his usual custom.

After that came a big dinner, and then a half hour spent with the funnies. Suddenly he dropped the newspaper as if its pages were charged with electricity.

"Wow!"

"What's wrong, Dan?" his Mother inquired from across the room.

"I forgot something important. I've got to rush out to Terry Treuhaft's place right away!"

"Can't it wait?"

Dan shook his head and explained about the broken window. "I promised the Cubs I'd take care of it first thing today, Mom. It sort of slipped my mind. I'll go right now."

He fished two precious dollar bills from his bank. The window shouldn't cost half that much, he hoped. But to be on the safe side, he would take an extra dollar along.

"Do you want your father to drive you to the cottage?" his mother questioned.

"I don't mind walking," Dan replied. "See you later."

Leaves were falling fast, dotting walks and high-

Payment Refused

way. Dan shuffled through them, enjoying the soft crackle underfoot. He sucked in a deep breath, and then began to whistle because his spirits were high.

Terry Treuhaft was nowhere about when Dan came to the cottage. He rapped on the door. The knock was a bit more forceful than he had intended it to be.

Almost at once the door was opened by a stout woman in a checkered dress. Dan assumed she must be Mrs. Treuhaft and he could guess by the expression of her face that she was very annoyed.

"I'm sorry," he apologized quickly. "I didn't mean to knock so hard."

Mrs. Treuhaft did not smile or reply graciously as he had expected her to do. Instead, she fixed him with an unfriendly stare.

"What do you want?" she asked, not opening the door very wide.

Dan explained that he had come to see Mr. Treuhaft.

"He isn't here and won't be for awhile," the woman answered shortly.

Dan reached for his pocketbook. "I want to pay for the window at the church," he said. "Do you think a dollar will be enough?"

"Church window?" A strange light flickered in Mrs. Treuhaft's steel gray eyes.

Dan started to tell her what had happened the previous day, but she cut him short.

"You think a dollar is enough to pay for the damage! Well, the very idea!"

"It was only a small window," Dan said, startled by the intensity of the woman's outburst. "But I'll pay whatever you think it will cost to replace the glass. Two dollars maybe?"

"Two dollars! Why that wouldn't begin to do it. The damage was enormous! Simply enormous! My husband was furious when he learned of it. For your information, he's talking to the church trustees about it now."

Dan could not understand why such a fuss was being made about a window pane. Hadn't he offered to pay? Why, the incident was being blown up out of all proportion!

"You have a nerve coming here and offering me a dollar!" the woman went on angrily. "But it proves one thing. You admit you did the damage?"

"Why, yes, we broke the window. It was an accident. We were playing with a basketball and it went wild, through the glass."

Payment Refused

"That's all I want to know." The woman nodded with grim satisfaction and closed the door in Dan's face.

A moment later she flung it open again to add severly: "You'll hear more about this later!"

Then she closed the door again.

Puzzled by the woman's strange behavior, Dan started slowly home. He was sorely troubled to learn that the Treuhafts meant to make so much of the accident. What sum, he wondered, could they demand for a broken window? If two dollars wasn't enough to pay for the glass, he'd really have to dig deep into his savings.

"Why, when I drove a baseball through Mrs. Simpson's basement window last Spring she charged me only seventy-five cents," he reflected. "I guess a church window must be something special. But that window wasn't stained glass—just ordinary."

Dan decided not to tell Chub how much the mishap was to cost. He was quite sure the new Cub had little or no spending money and couldn't be expected to help out in any case. Anyway, he'd offered to pay for the damage. Since the money had been refused, the next move would be up to Mr. Treuhaft.

Dan Carter and the Cub Honor

Monday night when Dan went to the church gymnasium for basketball practice, he still was brooding about the unfortunate accident. However, he did not disturb the other boys by relating what had happened. The Cubs tried free throws and worked out a team play which didn't go too smoothly.

Finally, everyone went upstairs for a special meeting Mr. Hatfield had called. Though the business session had been set for four-thirty sharp, the leader had not yet arrived. This was unusual, for Mr. Hatfield made a point of punctuality.

The boys talked over interesting places they had thought up for the Den to visit. As time dragged on and still Mr. Hatfield did not come, Brad tried to keep the Cubs interested by discussing plans for the Friday night party.

"Anyone found an ice cream freezer yet?" he asked the group.

"We know there are a couple at the old church," Midge finally said. "We should be able to get those."

"Don't count on it," Dan interposed. "Old Terry Treuhaft has it in for us. He's really steaming."

"Terry's down on the Cubs?" Brad questioned in surprise. "Why?"

Payment Refused

The Cubs looked embarrassed, reluctant to explain. When Brad pressed his inquiry, Chub stammered:

"It—it was all my fault. I threw a basketball through the church window."

"The blame was partly mine, and I'm paying for it," Dan said quickly. "I went out to Treuhaft's place yesterday. He wasn't there and his wife was pretty snippy with me. So I figure we won't get those freezers now."

"There must be others in Webster City. But we'll have to hustle if we get them in time for Friday. Guess I'd better name a special committee to look after the job and see that the ice cream is ready in time for the party. Any volunteers?"

"I'll do my best," Dan offered.

"Good! I'll appoint Chub, Red and Chips to help you. Fred and Midge are to look up the matter of getting ice and rock salt. Mrs. Holloway has promised to help with the ice cream mixture. What kind'll we have?"

"Tutti fruiti," piped up Chips.

"You would think of something like that, you drip!" Midge accused. "We're having something simple like vanilla."

41

"Let's compromise on strawberry," Brad suggested. "All in favor, say 'aye.' Opposed? The ayes have it."

By this time it was ten minutes to five, and the Cubs began to shift uneasily in their chairs. Mr. Hatfield never had been so late before.

"I'll bet he's been in an auto accident," Chips began to speculate. "Something has happened or he'd be here."

"I could telephone his house," Brad said reluctantly.

He was debating the matter when the Cubs heard an outside church door open and close.

"There he is now," Brad exclaimed in relief.

Mr. Hatfield came into the meeting room, his gaze sweeping the semi-circle of expectant Cubs.

"I am sorry to be late, boys." He spoke stiffly, and in an oddly subdued tone of voice.

The Cubs knew instantly that something was wrong. Mr. Hatfield didn't seem at all his usual pleasant, easy-going self. His lips were drawn into a tight line of disappointment and he was unsmiling.

"We thought something had happened to you," Brad remarked. "Shall we start the meeting with a song or the pledge of allegiance?"

Payment Refused

"No, it's too late for a meeting now," Mr. Hatfield replied. "We have a very important matter to discuss."

The Cubs became most attentive, aware that for some reason the group had incurred the leader's displeasure. As Mr. Hatfield's gaze swept the semicircle it lingered for a moment on Dan. The boy had an uncomfortable feeling that he was being singled out for attention. Had Old Terry Treuhaft complained about the window perhaps?

"Boys, I've just come from an unpleasant meeting," Mr. Hatfield said. "I was on my way here when I received a telephone call, asking me to stop at the office of Richard W. Brady."

"The lawyer?" interposed Brad, recognizing the name.

Mr. Hatfield nodded and went on: "Mr. Brady represents the trustees of the Christian Church."

Dan felt a cold lump come into his throat. So his hunch had been right! Old Terry Treuhaft had made trouble about the window.

"I've had a most uncomfortable half hour," Mr. Hatfield resumed. "Mr. Brady has accused our organization of some very dishonorable acts. To put it concisely, he's threatening to sue for $20,000!"

CHAPTER 5

A THREATENING SUIT

MR. HATFIELD'S blunt announcement electrified the Cubs. For a moment no one spoke and then there was a buzz of excited conversation. Everyone talked at the same time, demanding details.

"I can't tell you very much," Mr. Hatfield replied. "Mr. Brady said two of the church trustees came to him this morning, asking that he place their complaint before the Scout organization. The trustees insist that Cub Scouts visited the church grounds Saturday and did a great deal of damage. They demand a settlement of their claim, or they'll sue."

"Twenty thousand for a broken window?" Dan demanded. "Why, that's crazy!"

"Those old trustees are out of their heads!" Red added furiously.

"More than a single window is involved," Mr. Hatfield informed the Cubs. "Statues were broken, the attorney said, and at least three of the large stained-glass windows."

"But that's impossible!" Dan cried.

"We only broke one tiny little window," Red added.

A Threatening Suit

"Start at the beginning and tell me everything," Mr. Hatfield ordered. "Who went out to the church Saturday?"

"I planned the hike," Dan confessed. "Brad and Fred couldn't go. Chips, Chub, Midge, Red and myself were the only ones."

"You were after an ice cream freezer the attorney said."

"That's right. We asked Mr. Treuhaft if we could borrow a couple that are stored in the basement. He was busy and told us to come back later."

"After he turned you down, did you try to break into the church?"

"We certainly didn't," Dan denied indignantly.

"We just ate lunch there and tossed my basketball around a little while," Red contributed. "Chub made a bad throw and broke a window. That's all there was to it, except that Dan said he'd pay for it."

"I tried," Dan took up the story. "Yesterday I went to Old Terry's place. He wasn't there, but his wife refused the money."

"Has anyone returned to the church since the group left there Saturday?" the Cub leader inquired.

"I went past once on my way from Mr. Treuhaft's place," Dan answered. "That was Sunday."

"Did you see anyone around the premises?"

"Why, no." The question surprised Dan. "No person," he amended. "I did see a sort of shadow moving away toward the graveyard. It might have been a person or an animal or—"

"Or a ghost?" interposed Midge, half teasingly.

The other Cubs however, were in no mood for his joke.

"How could the trustees threaten to sue for twenty thousand dollars?" Brad asked, deeply troubled. "Why, it's silly! Anyway, they haven't a chance of collecting, because we don't have twenty dollars, much less twenty thousand."

"They're threatening to bring a court action against the entire Scout organization," Mr. Hatfield explained. "The Scout treasury by coincidence has almost exactly twenty thousand. The money is in a special building fund."

"Mr. Brady knew that!" Dan exploded. "That's why he's demanding so much."

"Perhaps," the Cubmaster agreed. "But any way we look at it, this is serious business. The honor of our Den is at stake."

"How can they blame us for something we didn't do?" Midge demanded.

A Threatening Suit

Mr. Hatfield assured the Cubs that he believed their story that only one window had been broken.

"I'm driving out to the church now to see for myself how much damage has been done," he announced. "Who wants to ride along?"

Because it was nearing the dinner hour, only Brad, Dan, Fred and Chips elected to go.

The sun was riding low in the sky by the time the automobile reached the church grounds. Mr. Hatfield parked along the main road, and the boys walked up the broken front walk.

"Twenty thousand, of course, is a ridiculous figure to demand," Mr. Hatfield remarked, following the Cubs. "I doubt the property is worth much more than that, including the land. The trustees have been trying to sell it for nearly two years, and haven't yet found a buyer."

"So they're taking it out on us!" Chips said resentfully.

The walk curved and the Cubs obtained a clear view of the old building. Dan, slightly ahead of the others, halted abruptly, dismayed by what he saw.

Not one, but half a dozen small windows had been smashed. The rainbow-hued glass of a circular, stained window had been broken too.

"Someone else did that!" he exclaimed. "No wonder the trustees are sore!"

"It's unfair to blame the Cubs," Chips declared.

The boys circled the old church, noting evidence of extensive damage. With so many windows smashed, entry into the building itself could not be prevented.

Chips started to crawl through one of the larger openings, but Mr. Hatfield hauled him back.

"We're in deep enough now," he said severely. "Don't make it worse."

It was well that Chips was prevented from crawling through the window, for a few minutes later, an automobile pulled up at the side entrance of the building.

Terry Treuhaft and two men the Cubs did not recognize, came over to the group.

"The church trustees, I think," Mr. Hatfield advised in a whisper.

His guess was correct. The two elderly men proved to be Elwin Maxwell and Joshia Brennan. The newcomers spoke curtly to Mr. Hatfield and ignored the Cubs completely.

Old Terry unlocked the front church door with a massive key so that the trustees could enter. Though

A Threatening Suit

not invited to do so, the Cubs followed close behind.

In the vestibule a marble statue lay smashed. Plaster either had fallen of its own weight or had been knocked in ugly patches from the walls. Pews were overturned, a stair railing broken from its supports and a stack of old hymn books scattered.

"You see what they did!" Old Terry said to the two trustees. "I've been taking good care of this place. Now look at it!"

"We had nothing to do with this," Dan said, trying to draw the attention of the trustees. "Absolutely nothing."

"These were the boys," Old Terry identified them for his employers. "They came out to my place to demand the key so they could get an ice cream freezer. When I denied it to 'em, they came here just the same and broke in."

"We came here to eat our lunch on the grounds," Dan replied, "but we didn't break in."

"You admit you broke a window?"

"One window. We didn't do all this damage."

"You were seen breaking in," Old Terry insisted. "Some folks in the neighborhood saw your gang climbing through the windows and called the police. But you managed to get away before the wagon came."

Dan Carter and the Cub Honor

"You must have dreamed all that!" Chip gasped.

"What time was this supposed to have happened?" Dan demanded.

"You know well enough. Just about dusk."

"We were home long before that," Chips retorted. "So your story doesn't hang together."

Mr. Hatfield spoke quietly. "The Cubs have told me their version of what happened, and I believe it. Den 2 boys are honorable and truthful. I'm convinced they're not responsible for this damage. Believe me, if I thought otherwise, I'd be the last to defend them."

"You'll have an opportunity to defend them in court," Mr. Maxwell said acidly. "I don't care to discuss this matter further. See our attorney, Mr. Brady."

Mr. Hatfield knew that it would be a waste of breath to try to talk to the two trustees while they were in their present mood. He motioned for the Cubs to leave the church.

All filed out with exception of Brad, who had taken no part in the conversation with the trustees. He had busied himself at the rear of the church, inspecting an overturned pew which had caught his attention.

A Threatening Suit

"Coming, Brad?" Mr. Hatfield asked.

"Be right with you," the Den Chief replied.

Even then he lingered for a moment. When finally he came outside, he seemed very thoughtful.

"What's the matter, Brad?" Dan questioned him. "You're so quiet. You don't think we wrecked the church do you?"

"Of course not."

"You're acting sort of queer. What kept you in the church, Brad? You were looking at that bench a long while."

"I found something too."

"You did?" Dan became eager. "What was it, Brad? Anything that might help clear the Cubs?"

"I don't know," Brad replied slowly. "It might not have any significance, and then again, it could."

"What did you find?"

"You'll keep it under your hat?"

"Of course."

Brad lowered his voice. "On that overturned pew I noticed some freshly carved initials. They were 'P.O.' Does that mean anything to you?"

CHAPTER 6

A CHALLENGE FROM PAT

"'P. O.,'" Dan thoughtfully repeated the intials. "The only thing that pops into my mind is Post Office."

"That's hardly what I meant," Brad replied, smiling. "The letters were freshly carved. I could tell from the color of the wood. Besides, there were tiny splinters on the floor."

Dan surged with excitement as he realized the importance of the Den Chief's discovery. Since the initials had been cut so recently, it must mean that they had been carved by the person or persons who had wrecked the church.

"I know of only one person with the initials 'P. O.'," Brad said significantly. "Can't you guess?"

"Not Pat Oswald?"

"Who else? Of course we have no proof."

"Pat and his gang might have been here after the Cubs left last Saturday! Say, that could have been what happened! They wrecked the place and we get blamed."

A Challenge From Pat

"That's the way I figure it," Brad nodded. "But as I said, we have no proof."

"Let's tell the trustees."

"Thats for Mr. Hatfield to decide, Dan. This accusation against the Cubs is dead-serious business and we can't make any false moves. If we'd charge Pat with this, we might be called on to prove our claims. Could we do that?"

"Not yet, I guess."

"That's why we must keep a tight lip and see what we can learn."

Dan knew that Brad's reasoning was sound. Though they suspected Pat and the group of boys he ran with, they certainly could not prove it. Inquiry in the neighborhood, however, might bring to light additional clues.

Mr. Hatfield, unaware of Brad's discovery, was still talking to Old Terry and the trustees. His efforts to convince them of the Cubs' innocence was unavailing. The only concession that the church officials made was to agree that the Cubmaster might appear before the entire church board the following Wednesday.

Breaking off the conversation, the trustees drove away.

Old Terry, left behind, began to assert his authority.

"Now you boys get off this property!" he directed. "Haven't you caused enough trouble?"

"It's unfair to accuse us!" Chips said furiously. "We didn't do the damage, and you should know it! Cubs aren't hoodlums."

"You wanted that freezer, and you didn't care how many windows you smashed to get in!"

"That just isn't so," Dan declared. "We never did get the freezers. Like enough they're still in the basement. Have you looked."

"No, I haven't."

"Why don't you?" Chips demanded. "I guess that would prove—"

"It wouldn't prove anything," the caretaker retorted, locking the church door. "Now begone, will you?"

"Come along, boys," Mr. Hatfield said quietly. "No use arguing about this affair. Everything will be taken up at the meeting Wednesday."

Decidedly downcast, the Cubs followed their leader to the car. During the ride into Webster City, they assured him repeatedly that they were innocent of the charges against them.

A Challenge From Pat

"I believe you," Mr. Hatfield said. "Don't worry too much about it. I think—I hope at any rate—that everything can be explained and adjusted. Unfortunately, Elwin Maxwell is a very stubborn man."

"He's chairman of the board too, isn't he?" Brad recalled.

"Yes, I gather he is the one who is pressing the suit."

Even the thought of a twenty thousand dollar claim filed against the Scout organization dismayed the Cubs. If such action were taken, there would be unpleasant newspaper publicity and court sessions. The Cubs would be given a black-eye in the community. Even if they later were cleared, they might never completely live it down.

"How about the party for our folks Friday?" Dan presently asked. "Now that we're in this mess, shall we drop our plans?"

"Absolutely not, Dan."

"So far we haven't any ice cream freezers."

"We'll get them somewhere. If necessary, we'll buy ice cream at the drugstore. The party goes on exactly as planned."

The Cubs brightened at this decision and began to discuss ways and means of clearing themselves of the outrageous charge against them. Brad told of the discovery he had made inside the church.

"Pat Oswald," Mr. Hatfield mulled over the name. "I hadn't thought of him. Brad, you may have hit upon something!"

"Do you think it will clear the Cubs?"

"I'm afraid not, Brad. But at least it gives us a starting point for our own investigation." Mr. Hatfield stopped the car for a traffic light. Shifting gears to go on, he added: "Now, we must say nothing about finding the carved initials, boys. But see what information you can pick up about Pat and his gang."

"Pat is known as a troublemaker," Chips declared.

"We'll need facts, not hearsay," Mr. Hatfield reminded the boys. "By the way, when you fellows were out at the church Saturday, you didn't notice anyone loitering around?"

"Not actually," Dan said. "Chub thought he saw a ghost though. We rather made fun of him."

"Maybe what he saw was someone hiding in the bushes," Brad pointed out.

"That's so," Dan agreed. He hadn't intended to mention his own experience, but now decided to tell about seeing the shadowy figure slithering toward the graveyard.

A Challenge From Pat

He related the incident hesitantly, half expecting the Cubs to tease him. No one did.

"Obviously, you didn't see a ghost," Mr. Hatfield commented. "You probably caught a glimpse of one of those hoodlums, Dan."

"Funny thing though," Dan replied meditatively. "The shadow I saw didn't look like a boy ghost. The figure was rather tall and thin. I had the queerest feeling at the time, almost the same as I did today—"

"What do you mean, 'as you did today?'" Brad alertly tripped him up.

The remark had slipped from Dan unintentionally. He certainly didn't want the Cubs to think that he was jittery. Or that he was imagining things. He remained silent.

"Come on, give!" Brad commanded.

"It was nothing really."

"You did see someone again today at the church?"

"No," Dan answered. "It was just a feeling I had while we were in the church. You'll laugh I know, but I had the strangest feeling that we were being watched."

"Watched?" said Mr. Hatfield. "By whom?"

"I can't explain it. As I said, it was just a feeling.

I—I felt as if everything we said and did inside that building was being noted."

"That was imagination, I'm afraid," Mr. Hatfield smiled. "I can understand the feeling though. The church interior was quiet and filled with strange echoes. Don't give it too much thought Dan."

Feeling slightly rebuked, Dan made no mention of the incident of the tapping bell. Nor did Chips speak of it. Neither of them believed that there were ghosts either at the old church or anywhere.

One by one the Club leader dropped the boys off at their separate homes. He promised that the moment he had anything to report about the church matter he would call a special meeting.

Meanwhile, the Cubs continued to make plans for the Friday night ice cream party. Search as they would, however, they could not locate even a single ice cream freezer.

"No hope of getting those two in the church basement either," Dan gloomily remarked to Brad Tuesday night after school. The two boys stood at a street corner, books under their arms. "For that matter, I wouldn't even ask Old Terry to lend 'em now."

"He'd just turn us down," Brad agreed.

A Challenge From Pat

Unobserved by the two Cubs, Pat Oswald and a companion had come up behind them. As Dan turned he saw the pair and knew they deliberately had been listening.

"What's that about Old Terry?" Pat asked.

"Nothing," Dan replied shortly.

"Oh, I heard what you said. "You want to borrow an old ice cream freezer from him, and he won't let you have it."

"Anything wrong in wanting a freezer?" Brad asked pleasantly. "Maybe you know where we can get one."

"Maybe I do," Pat grinned. "But I wouldn't tell, not in a million years. I'd hate to be a Cub!"

"You'd hate to be one?" Dan demanded. Pat's manner irritated him. He disliked the older boy's smug smile and attitude of knowing-it-all. "Why?"

"Cubs are babies—little baby bears!"

"You don't know anything about the organization!"

"Don't I? Well, let me tell you a thing or two, Mr. Danny Boy Carter, everyone in Webster City has heard about the mess they're in now!"

Dan and Brad were chagrined by this thrust. So the story had spread that church authorities had threatened to sue!

"The Cubs are sunk!" Pat chortled. "By the time the court gets through, there won't be an organization left. It will serve you right, too, for wrecking the old church."

"We didn't do it, and you know it," Dan retorted. "Say, weren't you and your gang out that way last Saturday?"

"Who says so?" Pat returned, instantly on the defensive.

"You know plenty about what happened."

"Only what I heard," Pat replied. His bluster had faded away.

Dan was elated to note that his sharp question had worried the other. He would have pursued the matter further, but Pat and his friend moved off.

"You scored that time, Dan," Brad said when they were alone again. "All the same, go easy in talking to him. If we're to learn anything, we mustn't give away what we suspect."

"I'll be more careful," Dan promised. "Did you notice how he acted when I suggested that he'd been around the church Saturday."

"I did, Dan. Tomorrow night I'm going out there again, and canvass the neighborhood. It may be that we can dig up someone who saw the damage

A Challenge From Pat

being done. In that case, the Cubs could be cleared."

"Pat and his gang were responsible, I'll bet on that."

"I think so myself," Brad agreed. "But don't forget, we must prove any charges we make."

Though the Webster City newspapers carried only brief stories on the damage which had been done at the Christian Church, word of it spread very rapidly.

No mention had been made of the Cub organization or the threatened law suit in either the Webster City Herald or the Journal. Nevertheless, rumors circulated that the boys of Den 2 were responsible for the damage. The Cubs smarted under the humiliation.

"We'll never live this down," Midge said morosely the next afternoon as the Cubs waited in their clubroom.

Mr. Hatfield had called a special meeting and the boys were expecting him at any moment. He came in just then, so sober-faced that the Cubs instantly knew bad news awaited them.

"I've just come from talking to the church trustees," he reported after hanging up his hat on the wall rack. "Our meeting was to have been later, but our lawyer arranged an earlier conference."

"Our lawyer?" Brad asked, startled. "Do we have one?"

"The Scout organization has obtained the services of a very able attorney. We thought it best to employ counsel."

"Then this accusation against us is really serious?" Brad questioned. The other Cubs, deeply worried, had gathered about in a tight, tense little group.

"Yes, it's serious," Mr. Hatfield admitted drawing a deep breath. "As I started to tell you, our lawyer and some of the Scout officials talked to the trustees."

"Wouldn't they listen to reason?" Red inquired.

"No. Several of the board members were inclined to accept our word that the Cubs wouldn't and couldn't have destroyed church property. Maxwell wouldn't go along with the others. He's determined to sue unless we pay for the damage."

"Twenty thousand dollars," Chips muttered. "Why, that old wreck of a place isn't worth half that amount!"

"I'm afraid it is, Chips. However, a damage claim of twenty thousand is ridiculous. Mr. Maxwell him-

A Challenge From Pat

self recognizes that, for he has offered to settle for ten thousand if the organization pays within ten days."

"The old skinflint!" Red exclaimed.

"We've refused," Mr. Hatfield went on. "The next move is up to the trustees. All we can do is wait."

Now that the Cub leader's report had been made, the boys were in no mood for a long meeting. Brad took up a few matters concerning the Friday party, including the necessity for finding at least one ice cream freezer.

"Tomorrow is our last chance," he told the Cubs. "Everyone get busy. Ask friends and neighbors and let's see if we can't find one."

As Brad ended his little pep talk, the boys were startled to hear a loud pounding on the closed clubroom door.

Chub and Dan both jumped up to see who had rapped.

Dan reached the door first. No one was there. He thought though, that he heard a muffled snicker, and certainly he detected the sound of retreating footsteps. As he listened a moment, he noticed a folded piece of paper lying on the cement floor almost at his feet.

"What's that?" Chub cried, seeing the paper at the same instant.

Dan picked it up. He unfolded the coarse, soiled sheet to discover a pencil-scrawled message.

"THE CUBS ARE SISSIES," it read. "WE CAN LICK YOU IN BASKETBALL ANY OLD DAY. HOW ABOUT A GAME? THIS IS A CHALLENGE. LEAVE YOUR ANSWER IN A BOTTLE IN HAGERMAN'S ALLEY."

The note was signed "Pat Oswald and the Purple Five."

CHAPTER 7

"KNOW YOUR NEIGHBORHOOD"

AS Dan read the note from Pat, the Cubs' first reaction was one of annoyance.

"Why, the nerve of him!" Fred Hatfield exclaimed. "He sneaks up here, listens to our sessions, and then leaves a cheap challenge!"

"Let's write a hot note back, telling that Purple Five to go jump in an ash can!" Red proposed.

Dan and Brad dashed down the corridor to see if they could intercept the intruders. However, Pat and his followers had slipped out a side door and were nowhere in sight.

The two Cubs knew that it would be useless to search the church yard, so they rejoined the other boys in the meeting room. By this time, argument over the note had attained a high pitch.

Red, Fred and Chips were in favor of rejecting the challenge in short order. Chub held no opinion whatsoever. Midge was talking in favor of giving the dare serious consideration.

"If we refuse to play, Pat will go all over town,

saying we're afraid to do it because we'd be licked," he argued.

"We might at that," Brad interposed. "Our team isn't the smoothest on wheels."

"We haven't practiced much, that's why," Midge insisted. "Why, we could beat Pat and his hoodlums with our hands tied behind our backs!"

"I wouldn't be too sure of it myself," Brad said with an easy smile. "From what I hear, Pat is a first-rate athlete."

"We saw a sample of his basket shooting the other day," Dan reminded the Cubs.

"You think that stupid Purple Five team could beat us?" Red demanded, leaping to his feet. "Why, that's downright disloyal."

Dan hesitated to make his position clear. "I'm not saying any such thing, and I'm not disloyal, Red. Maybe our Cub team, disorganized as it is, could beat the Purple Five. Then again, maybe we couldn't. It might be an interesting match."

"What if they should lick us?" Chips asked uneasily.

"That's a risk we'd have to take," Brad answered. "Naturally, if we decide to play, we'll have to get busy and practice."

Know Your Neighborhood

Mr. Hatfield had taken no part in the discussion, and Dan now asked him what he thought of the challenge.

"First, let's hear your opinion, and then I'll speak my piece," the Cub leader replied.

"Well, I'm in favor of picking up the challenge," Dan replied after a moment of thought. "For two reasons. First, if we turn the game down, Pat and his gang will go around saying we're afraid of defeat. Then it hit me that if we really want to learn more about those kids and their habits, this would be a mighty good chance!"

"They're a bunch of hoodlums!" Red said resentfully. "It's probably their fault that the Scout organization is mixed up in a threatened lawsuit. They slap us on one cheek and we hold up another for a big wallop!"

"We only suspect that Pat's outfit did the damage at Christian Church," Brad said, supporting Dan's position. "If we schedule a game, we may overhear talk that will give us a straight lead. What do you think, Mr. Hatfield?"

"Cubs are supposed to give good will," he replied gravely. "Pat and his gang haven't had many advantages. Contact with a church, a worthwhile Cub organization and wholesome sportsmanship, might do the outfit a world of good."

"Sure, but what about us?" Red argued. Won't they make more and more trouble?"

"That's a possibility, Red. But I think the Cubs can look after themselves."

"So do I," declared Dan. "Let's arrange a game and then get busy and practice."

An animated discussion followed as the boys made their plans. Mr. Hatfield suggested that a series of three games be scheduled in the church gymnasium. He promised that they would be closely supervised and rules strictly enforced.

"How about charging admission?" Brad suggested. "If the Cub organization has to pay for the services of a lawyer, we should be getting some money in our treasury."

As a general rule, Mr. Hatfield did not favor selling tickets or charging admission for Cub affairs. Nevertheless, he acknowledged that the Den's need for cash was urgent and that a few extra dollars might be of great help.

"We might charge a small amount," he agreed reluctantly. "Twenty-five cents perhaps."

Only the date for the first game remained to be

Know Your Neighborhood

settled. Mr. Hatfield said he thought it should be set for at least ten days ahead to give the Cubs time to practice and better organize their team.

"We can't devote all our time to athletics," he warned the boys. "Remember, we have those 'Know Your Neighborhood' visits ahead, not to mention the party for parents. Speaking of the party, I'm ashamed to say I've been so busy with conferences, I've had no chance to try to look up ice cream freezers."

"No one can find any," Midge reported gloomily. "That party will be one big flop."

"Not at all," Mr. Hatfield cheered him. "I think that it might be well to postpone the affair one week. Another seven days will give us time enough to round up a freezer or two."

The Cubs were relieved by the change in plan, especially as everyone was in an uneasy mood regarding the outcome of the threatened lawsuit. After electing Dan captain of the basketball team, they assigned him and Brad to notify Pat Oswald that the challenge had been accepted.

"It's too silly, leaving a note in a bottle in an alley," Brad objected. "Why don't we just write an acceptance and mail it to his home."

The latter course was decided upon, and later that night the two boys composed the letter and sent it off. Two days later a message was returned to the church clubroom, accepting the first basketball game date and agreeing to the series of three contests.

"The deal is on, and now we've got to buckle down," Dan warned his teammates. "Gobs of practice!"

Determined not to be shown up by the Purple Five, the Cubs spent every spare hour in the church gymnasium.

Gradually, under the coaching of Brad, the team began to shape up. Dan and Midge, having the best eye for basket shooting, were assigned as forwards. Red and Chips, both being sturdily built, were to guard. Brad would play center, as he had a long reach, and was taller than any of the younger boys.

Chub and Fred were assigned as substitutes. Neither was very adept at handling a basketball. Both attended practice sessions faithfully, but Fred in particular had no deep interest in the game, preferring to read.

Mr. Hatfield attended the work-outs whenever he could. He was very busy, however, and fre-

Know Your Neighborhood

quently was summoned to special meetings with Scout leaders, court officials and attorneys. That the Cubmaster was deeply worried over the pending lawsuit was obvious from his preoccupied manner.

Though basketball had become an absorbing interest, Brad and Dan did not neglect other Cub activities. They made plans for "Know Your Neighborhood" visits, and launched the building of a cardboard fort in the clubroom. Fred enthusiastically took charge of the work, gathering materials and supervising the construction.

"We're pretty well set for our Mom and Dad's party, if only we had an ice cream freezer," Dan remarked one afternoon. "Mr. Hatfield intended to find one, but he's been too busy to give it any thought."

"Let's try to rustle it ourselves," Brad proposed. "How about a house to house canvas?"

"I've already tried almost every home in our block."

"We could work a new neighborhood, Dan. How about the locality of Old Christian Church?"

"Why there, Brad?"

"Thought we could do a little investigating at the same time. On the pretext of asking for an ice cream freezer, we can question folks in the neighborhood about whether or not there were any witnesses to the damage that was done."

"Not a bad idea," Dan approved.

The boys hiked to within a block of the old church and then began ringing doorbells. At each house they voiced a double inquiry. First they asked if an old fashioned ice cream freezer could be borrowed, and then they inquired for information regarding the recent trouble at the deserted building.

After nearly twenty unfruitful calls, Dan and Brad began to grow discouraged. No one it seemed had an ice cream freezer, and the only comment they obtained relative to the church damage was that "a group of Boy Scouts did it."

"No witnesses apparently," Brad said, losing heart. "It begins to look mighty bad for Den 2,, Dan."

"Let's try one more house," Dan suggested.

The one he indicated stood directly across from the abandoned church. Purposely, the boys had left it to the last, so that their tour would end near a bus stop.

Going up the winding walk, Dan and Brad rapped on the door. A man in shirt-sleeves, a news-

Know Your Neighborhood

paper in his hand, came to the door. The two boys repeated their inquiries which by now had become a routine speech.

"I don't know where you can find an ice cream freezer," the man turned them down. He stared at the blue uniforms which the boys wore. "Say, you boys are Cub Scouts, aren't you?"

"Yes, we are," Dan replied proudly.

"Were you in the gang that was supposed to have ripped the church building apart?"

"We were not," Dan returned. "Our organization has been falsely accused. We're trying to prove we had nothing to do with it."

"Can't you?"

"It's not so easy. You see, a few of us visited the grounds before the real damage was done. We accidentally smashed a window. After we left, the place was wrecked, and we were accused."

"It happened just after dark," the home owner said. "I know because I heard windows being smashed. A half dozen kids, more or less, were in the gang, running wild over the place. I called police, but they got away before the wagon arrived."

"Did you see any of the boys?" Brad asked eagerly.

"Only at a distance."

"You didn't see anyone in Cub uniforms?"

"I was too far away to tell. The boys mostly were large fellows. Too old to be Cubs, I'd judge."

Brad and Dan asked the man for his name and address, intending to give it to Mr. Hatfield. If their case actually came to trial it might be that he could be called to testify in behalf of the Cubs. His information, though, was meager.

After leaving the house, the two boys went across the street to peer at the church building again. Since their last visit, all the windows had been repaired.

"Not too much damage has been done." Brad said, gazing about. "Those trustees are just trying to build up a big case without much to go on."

Dan pressed his face against a basement window, peering down into the storage room.

"Those freezers are still there," he announced. "I sure wish we could borrow 'em for the party."

"Well, we can't," Brad returned. "I wouldn't ask those trustees for a favor, even if we never find a freezer."

"Here either," Dan agreed. "Say, I see our bus coming. Let's grab it."

During the next two days, the Cubs were kept very busy at school. Each afternoon was spent in

Know Your Neighborhood

the gymnasium. On several occasions, they saw members of Pat's crowd watching from the windows. The boys never would come inside, but plainly were studying the game and tactics of the Cubs.

"They're trying to study out our plays," Dan reported to his teammates. "Well, let 'em. We'll beat them fair and square."

On Saturday morning, Mr. Hatfield took all Den members to Juvenile Court on the first visit scheduled in the "Know Your Neighborhood" series of excursions.

The boys watched a hearing in progress, listened to a little talk on traffic safety, and then met a judge.

Later, they crossed a corridor to another cluster of offices. Mr. Hatfield explained that private hearings were conducted for boys and girls who had committed misdemeanors. He led the Cubs into the office of Harold Greene, court director.

"Boys, I want you to meet an old friend of mine," he introduced them.

The Cubs were grateful that the Juvenile Court official made no reference whatsoever to the incident involving the old Christian Church. He knew about it, they were certain, but purposely was being tactful.

Mr. Greene shook hands with each Cub in turn. When he came to Chub, he nodded and smiled and said:

"Why, Chub, I'm glad to see you again. Getting along fine, aren't you?"

"Yes, sir," Chub mumbled nervously.

"You like the place where you are living now?"

"Y-yes, sir," Chub muttered again. He seemed very ill at ease and acted relieved when Mr. Hatfield steered the boys on to another office.

The Cubs could not fail to note that Chub was well known to the Court director. Was it possible, they speculated, that at some time he had been before the court? Could that explain why Mr. Hatfield had warned them not to inquire into the boy's past?

The Cubs moved on to a public reception room where juveniles sat while awaiting calls to the conference chambers. Glancing carelessly over the group of downcast boys slouched in the chairs, Dan received another shock.

There in one of the chairs by the door, sat Pat Oswald! Seeing the Cubs, he quickly lowered his head into a magazine and pretended to read.

CHAPTER 8

A WISH FULFILLED

KNOWING that he had been recognized, Pat grinned sheepishly at Dan.

"I'm here with a friend of mine," he muttered "These birds haven't got anything on me—no sir!"

Dan had his own idea of why Pat might be in court, but he pretended to accept the explanation. He had heard at school that a group of boys had been loitering near the railroad tracks, boarding freight trains, and otherwise making a nuisance of themselves. Undoubtedly, Pat and some of his cronies had been brought in by police for questioning.

This was confirmed a moment later as one of the court referees came out of his private office and motioned to Pat.

"I'll talk to you next," he said "Come in."

Pat cast a quick look at Dan, and ducked into the conference room.

The tour of the big courthouse continued. Dan could not fail to note that Chub seemed rather familiar with the Juvenile Court section of the building. More than ever he was convinced that the new Cub member was known to some of the referees as well as the court director. Chub, however, maintained his usual shy silence and offered no explanation.

The boy's familiarity with the building did not escape the attention of the other Cubs. As they were leaving after the tour, Red sidled over to Dan.

"What do you think about Chub?" he whispered.

"Nothing, why?"

"Did you notice how the court director knew him?"

"Sure, but what of it?"

"Well—" Red was rather ashamed of his own suspicions. "I just wonder if maybe he hasn't been in some trouble—"

"I wouldn't do too much speculating," Dan said to end the talk. "Don't you like Chub?"

"Sure, but—"

"No buts then, Red. Mr. Hatfield told us Chub was okay, and that's enough for me."

"Same here," Red shrugged. "I was just thinking, that's all."

During the next few days the Cubs devoted many hours to basketball practice. When not otherwise oc-

A Wish Fulfilled

cupied they worked on the cardboard fort in the meeting room and perfected plans for the coming Friday night party.

The problem of finding an ice cream freezer still confronted the Cubs. On Thursday, only a day before the scheduled affair to honor parents, the boys admitted that they were up against it.

"We'll have to buy our ice cream," Brad said to the Den members as they sat discussing the matter in their clubroom. "Mr. Hatfield has been too busy to do anything about finding a freezer, and the rest of us have had no luck."

"The party won't be any good without homemade ice cream," Midge said gloomily. "I wanted to turn the freezer too!"

"No use moaning about it," Brad replied. "We'll have a good party just the same. At any rate we'll have the big fort on display. Fred and his helpers did a fine job building it."

"Thanks," Fred said, warming to the praise. "It was a lot of work making the thing."

The fort, constructed of cut and painted sheets of cardboard, was a replica of an old pioneer historical building which the boys had visited several months before. Fred had spent weeks on the task, working out every detail with care. Now the structure was finished, ready for display at the Friday party.

"By the way, there's one business matter to come before the group," Brad resumed. "We have a request to consider from Pat Oswald."

"He wants to cancel the game!" Chips guessed.

"Quite the contrary. He and his boys are taking the tournament very seriously. Pat demands a chance to practice in our gymnasium before the game."

A silence fell upon the room. Then Red said grumpily: "Maybe he'd like to have us turn over the whole place to him!"

"The request seemed like a reasonable one."

Dan spoke up. "I think we should agree to let them use the gym. That is, if Mr. Hatfield says it is all right. The church gym wasn't built for our special use."

"Pat doesn't go to this church," Red growled. "He doesn't attend any church. Do him good if he did!"

"Cubs are supposed to be FAIR," Dan reminded him. "We agreed to a series of three games. Now do we want it to be an honest test of athletic skill, or do we want to win at any cost?"

A Wish Fulfilled

"Oh, let 'em use the gym," Red gave in, knowing all the other Cubs favored Brad's viewpoint. "Someone ought to keep watch though, while they're here. They might decide to wreck the place, the way they did the old church."

"That hasn't been proven," Brad said. "Anyway, you may be sure adults will supervise the practice closely."

Chub, who had been seated nearest the door, suddenly jumped up.

"What's wrong?" Midge asked him. "You're as nervous as a cat."

"I—I thought I heard someone in the hall."

"Maybe it's Mr. Hatfield coming," Brad said, glancing at the wall clock. "He's a tiny bit late again. Probably another meeting with Mr. Maxwell's lawyer."

The Cubs waited a moment, listening. Mr. Hatfield did not appear, but Dan thought he heard an outside door softly close.

"Maybe Pat and his gang have been eavesdropping again!" he cried.

The Cubs ran out into the shadowy corridor. It was quite deserted. But there against the wall, neatly positioned like twin sentinels, were two large ice cream freezers.

"Whoopee!" chortled Midge. "See what Santa Claus brought us!"

"Freezers!" Chips laughed, cavorting around them. "Just when we had given up hope too."

While the other Cubs were examining the mysterious gifts, Dan and Brad hastened on to the outer door.

They reached it in time to catch a fleeting glimpse of someone vanishing into a clump of bushes to the left of the churchyard.

"That wasn't Mr. Hatfield, was it?" Dan demanded.

"Too tall," Brad replied. "Anyway, he wouldn't have left the freezers in the hallway."

"Maybe it was one of the Den Dads. Odd though, that whoever it was, didn't rap on the clubroom door and wait to be thanked. Anyway, I'm sure glad to get those freezers!"

Brad kept frowning thoughtfully as he walked back to rejoin the other Cubs.

"Anything to show who left the freezers?" he asked Midge. "Any card?"

"Not a thing. They're big ones though. Just what we need for our party tomorrow night."

Dan too had been inspecting the freezers. He

A Wish Fulfilled

remarked that they were the same size as the ones he had noticed in the old Christian Church basement. "Do you suppose they came from there?" he speculated.

"I doubt it," Midge answered carelessly. "Those old trustees haven't relented one bit. And Terry wouldn't bring them to us—you know that."

"Well, we have 'em and that's what counts," Chips cheerfully declared. "Now we can go ahead with our plans. Let's make the ice cream first thing after school tomorrow night. It should keep if we pack it in ice."

Jubilantly, the Cubs carried the two freezers into the clubroom. They were still discussing the strange manner of delivery when Mr. Hatfield arrived. He had nothing new to report regarding the threatened damage suit, but expressed amazement that the Den had acquired the cream freezers.

"I had nothing to do with it," he assured the Cubs. "To be sure, I've asked a number of people if they knew where we could get some freezers. Perhaps one of our inquiries paid off."

Brad told the Cubmaster of the request Pat Oswald had made with reference to use of the gymnasium for a basketball practice session.

"No reason why they can't use it for an hour tomorrow night after school, is there?" Mr. Hatfield inquired. "The Cubs will be making ice cream and won't want the floor themselves."

"Do you think they should be allowed the run of the place?" Red protested. "You know how Pat and his gang are."

"The practice will be a supervised one. I promise you that," Mr. Hatfield said. "I see no reason why the boys shouldn't be allowed privileges here, providing they don't abuse them."

"You're forgetting how they got us into trouble," Red asserted.

"No, Red. I just believe in fair play, that's all. We agreed to the series of games, so it's only right that we give the Purple Five a chance to practice Right?"

"Oh, I guess so," Red submitted. "I don't trust Pat, that's all."

Word was carried to Pat that his team might use the gymnasium the following afternoon from three-thirty until four-thirty.

"You mean it?" The boy demanded in surprise when Dan gave him the information. "Well, thanks!"

"Say, by the way, you weren't at the church a

A Wish Fulfilled

while ago, were you?" Dan asked in an offhand way.

The moment he had asked the question, he regretted it. Once the words had been spoken it was too late to retract them.

"Why, no, why?" Pat demanded.

"Oh, a couple of ice cream freezers were delivered to the Cubs," Dan explained reluctantly. "I thought you might know something about it."

Pat's blank expression convinced Dan that he knew nothing of the matter. More than ever, he was sorry he had brought up the subject.

"What are the Cubs doing with ice cream freezers?" Pat demanded, his curiosity aroused. "For that party you're giving tomorrow night, I bet!"

Dan had not suspected that the other knew of the planned social affair.

"How'd you find out about it?" he asked.

Pat grinned provokingly. "That's for me to know and you to find out!" he retorted.

Thrusting hands deep into the pockets of his patched jeans, he sauntered off.

CHAPTER 9

STRAWBERRY ICE CREAM

"KEEP turning that crank! Do you want the paddles to stick?"

The irate command was directed by Red Suell at Chips who had rested a moment as he cranked one of the big ice cream freezers.

All of the Cubs except Brad were making ice cream in the church basement. Mrs. Holloway and Red's mother had volunteered to direct the work. The two mothers had been kept busy offering suggestions, for none of the boys ever before had made ice cream except in the tray of a refrigerator.

Dan and Midge had cracked the ice in a gunny sack, hammering the stubborn chunks until they were of tiny, uniform size. The metal containers, with their wooden paddles, had been set into the packed freezers, and now the cranking had begun. Red was assigned to one, while Chub and Chips took turns at the other.

"My arm is getting tired," Red complained. "Someone else take over!"

"You've hardly been at it two minutes," Dan

Strawberry Ice Cream

teased. Nevertheless, he seized the crank, turning it steadily and smoothly.

"Say, it's going harder and harder," he presently admitted. "Do you suppose the cream could be frozen?"

"Very nearly so," declared Mrs. Holloway, packing more ice into the freezer.

Dan kept cranking. Melted salt water spilled faster and faster out of the little round hole in the freezer.

"This is getting awfully hard!" he gasped, exerting all of his strength to keep the crank moving.

"And this old freezer is stuck!" cried Chips, who was taking his turn at the other freezer. "It won't budge an inch!"

"Shall we take a look?" asked Mrs. Holloway, relieving him.

She unfastened the top of the freezer, carefully opening the metal cylinder packed deep in ice. The Cubs clustered around, eager to see what their labors had produced.

Mrs. Holloway lifted the paddle slightly. The Cubs uttered squeals of delight. The wooden paddle was simply loaded with rich looking, delicately pink strawberry ice cream.

"It looks lovely, doesn't it?" Mrs. Holloway laughed. "Now you boys must draw straws to see who gets to lick the paddle!"

Chub won, so Mrs. Holloway handed the richly coated paddle to him on a paper plate. Midge was awarded the paddle from the freezer Dan had turned so faithfully.

"Gee, is this ever good!" he shouted, smacking his lips. "I wish I could have a big dish."

"You can tonight," Mrs. Holloway promised.

The other Cubs looked so downcast to see Midge and Chub eating the ice cream that Mrs. Holloway gave them each a tiny sample.

"Best ice cream I ever tasted," declared Dan. "I'll bet our party will be a huge success tonight."

Under the direction of the two mothers, the Cubs cleaned up the muss they had made in the basement. Both freezers then were packed firmly with chopped ice, so that the cream would remain solid until it was needed.

"Dan, I wish you and Red would help carry the freezers upstairs," Mrs. Holloway requested. "It's so warm here, the ice will melt. I think it will be better to set the freezers outside."

The two Cubs followed instructions, setting the

Strawberry Ice Cream

containers on a tiny back porch behind the church kitchen. To further protect them, they covered both freezers with a piece of canvas.

"Everything's set now for the party," Dan remarked cheerfully. "Wonder what's doing in the gym?"

Moving down the corridor, the two Cubs could hear the slap-slap-slap of rubber-soled shoes on the polished gymnasium floor. Brad, Mr. Hatfield and the other Cubs were there, watching the workout of the Purple Five.

Obviously, Pat and his players were trying to put on a show. They made a great commotion, passing the ball fast, executing rapid turns and pivots and taking long shots at the baskets. In a surprising number of instances, the ball found its mark.

"Say, they're plenty good," Dan admitted in a whisper. "Especially Pat."

"Watch 'em guard," Red replied, looking worried "Rough as all get-out."

Mr. Hatfield too, had observed the rough manner in which the boys played. As the practice session wound up, he remarked to Pat that it might be well for the Purple Five to study the rules before the first scheduled game.

"We play strictly according to the book," he warned. "Any unnecessary roughness will go down as a foul."

"You don't have to worry about our team," Pat replied boastfully. "We know the rules from Z to A."

After ending the practice, the Bay Shore boys took their time in leaving the church. They roved the corridors, peered down into the basement, and even into the Cub's private clubroom.

One of the boys spied the cardboard fort which Fred had built. "Gee! Will you look at the playhouse!" he shouted.

Mr. Hatfield shooed the five wanderers out of the building. On the steps, Pat noticed the two ice cream freezers.

"When do we eat?" he demanded boisterously.

"You don't," Chips told him. "Thats' for our party tonight."

"Who is invited?"

"Only the parents of the Cubs."

"Well, have a good time," Pat said with a grin. "See you later."

He peered again at the ice cream freezers, helped himself to a chunk of ice, and sauntered off.

The party that night began early. Soon after seven

Strawberry Ice Cream

o'clock, the parents started to arrive. Dan, Fred and Chub were on the welcoming committee to greet everyone at the door. The other Cubs were stationed at various tables, ready to explain the various exhibits.

The fort which Fred had constructed drew a great deal of favorable comment. Several parents expressed the hope that the structure would be kept on display for a long while.

"Oh, we intend to use it," Fred assured the group of admirers. "We'll play Indian games and act out pioneer stuff. Maybe put on a little play."

The Cubs were a bit impatient for the singing, the promotion ceremonies and other events to end. Eyeing the array of chocolate, angel food and spice cakes on the long supper table, they scarcely could wait until the moment came to eat.

Dan noticed that Chub seemed rather downcast. Sidling over to the younger boy, he asked him what was wrong.

"Nothing," Chub mumbled.

"You're not having a good time."

"Yes, I am," Chub insisted. "Wonderful!"

"Well, you don't act like it. Your face is as long as a roller towel. What's eating you?"

"Nothing," Chub said again. And then he went on hurriedly: "It's only that—that all the other Cubs have a mother and Dad here tonight. I'm all alone."

"Sure, I know how you feel." Dan clumsily flung an arm around the younger boy's shoulders. "But don't you care."

He very much wanted to ask Chub about his mother and father. But recalling Mr. Hatfield's advice not to ask questions, he remained silent.

Presently, Mrs. Hatfield announced that supper would be served. The parents lined up for their decorated paper plates, napkins, silverware and big piece of homemade cake.

"We'll be ready to dish up the ice cream in a minute," Mrs. Hatfield advised Dan and Brad. "Will you boys please fetch the freezers?"

"Sure thing," Dan said eagerly.

He and Brad, together with Red who wanted to help, went out on the porch for the canvas-covered freezers.

Looking about, they could not see the containers anywhere.

"Say, what became of 'em?" Dan demanded.

"There's the canvas," Red noted. He pointed

Strawberry Ice Cream

to the covering which lay in a heap on the ground near the steps.

"Do you suppose Mr. Hatfield moved them?" Brad speculated. "Wait, I'll find out."

He rushed back into the church, to return a moment later with the Cub leader. Mr. Hatfield assured the boys that he had not touched either of the freezers.

"When I came this way about thirty minutes ago, both were here."

"Then someone has taken them!" Dan exclaimed.

"Who would do such a mean thing?" Red demanded. "Our party is ruined!"

Word spread like wildfire that the ice cream had been stolen. The other Cubs and some of the parents came out of the church to see for themselves.

"Say, I bet I know who took those freezers!" Chips cried.

"Who?" the others demanded.

"Pat Oswald and his gang."

"It's hardly fair to accuse them just because they used the gymnasium today," Mr. Hatfield said rather mildly.

"Pat knew about the freezers," Chips insisted. "He saw them here on the steps, and he asked about the party."

Brad, with a pocket flashlight, had been examining the soft earth near the church steps.

"I've found a lot of shoe marks," he called the attention of the Cubs to them. "Boys tracks, I'd judge by their size. Have you fellows been tramping around here today?"

"Haven't been off the walk or the porch," Dan said, and most of the Cubs gave a similar reply.

"Well, a gang of kids must have been here then," Brad declared. "See the tracks lead toward the hedge. Here, you can tell that something heavy was dragged over the ground."

"Maybe it was Pat and his gang!" Fred exclaimed. "Of all the mean ingratitude! We let 'em use our gym and equipment, and they repay us by stealing our ice cream!"

"We worked so hard to make it too!" Red added.

"We ought to call off our basketball games with 'em—that's what," Midge said indignantly.

Mr. Hatfield reminded the Cubs that they had no proof that the ice cream actually had been taken by Pat and his cronies.

"It looks highly suspicious," he admitted, "but I'm in favor of giving the other fellow the benefit of the doubt."

Strawberry Ice Cream

Several of the Den Dads toured the church yard, in search of the culprits. They returned to report no sign of the freezers, or the persons who had taken them. Evidently the theft had been accomplished nearly a half hour earlier, or at least long before the discovery of the loss.

"No chance of catching anyone now," Mr. Hatfield said regretfully. "We may as well forget about it."

"Forget it?" Midge wailed. "After all the work we did?"

"And you never tasted such wonderful ice cream," Chips went on. "We only had tiny samples this afternoon. We were looking forward to big dishes tonight!"

"We'll make ice cream another time," Mr. Hatfield promised the Cubs.

"How can we, without freezers?" Dan asked. "The only ones we know about are at the old Christian Church. No chance of getting those."

"And what about the ones that were stolen?" Brad asked, rather worried. "We don't even know to whom they belong."

The Cubs had inquired among the parents, but no one had admitted providing the two freezers.

Even Mr. Hatfield was somewhat uneasy to think that later on, the unknown giver might call at the church to ask the return of his or her property.

"It's very strange about those freezers—" he mused. "Very strange."

Disconsolately, the Cubs trooped back into the church. They were resigned to a party without ice cream.

However, Midge's father had slipped away to the drugstore without consulting anyone. Even before all the cake had been served, he was back with several large packages of ice cream. He also had bought some excellent strawberry topping.

"Now this isn't as good as homemade ice cream," he apologized. "On short notice though, it was the best substitute I could find."

The Cubs ate their share of the ice cream and after a while tended to forget the injustice that had been done them. It relieved their minds to see that the parents didn't seem to mind not having homemade ice cream. Despite the theft of the freezers, the party had been a great success.

"Now before we break up for the evening, I suggest we give the Cubs a big vote of thanks," proposed Mr. Holloway. "All in favor—"

Strawberry Ice Cream

No one ever had an opportunity to join in the vote of appreciation. For at that moment there came a rap on the clubroom door.

Before anyone could open it, Terry Treuhaft stepped into the room. The old caretaker's unexpected arrival startled everyone. No one could imagine what had brought him to the church uninvited.

Terry did not long leave the matter in doubt.

"I've come for my freezers," he said and his voice fairly dripped icicles.

"YOUR freezers?" Red echoed. "Oh m'gosh!"

"I think you must be mistaken about us having your freezers," Mr. Hatfield said politely.

"We haven't any freezers at all," declared Chips, rather enjoying the joke.

"I understand you do have the ones that were at the church," the old caretaker said stiffly. "I was tipped that I'd find them here. Where are they?"

"Look around if you like," Brad invited. "If you can find them, you're better at hunting than we are."

"None of your sass, young man or I'll have the law on you," Old Terry retorted. He felt ill at ease with so many parents gazing steadily at him.

"I'm sorry," Brad apologized. "I did not intend to be impolite. I merely meant to emphasize that we do not have your freezers."

"You did have them then."

"That might be," Mr. Hatfield admitted. "We did have a couple of ice cream freezers which were stolen earlier tonight. However, I certainly had no suspicion that they belonged to the Christian Church."

"Well, you know now," Old Terry retorted. "These Cubs were after those freezers from the first, and that was what caused 'em to break in—"

"Just a minute," interposed Mr. Hatfield. "The Cubs did not break into the Church. Of that I'm satisfied."

"You may be satisfied, but the trustees aren't! The Cubs will have to pay for the damage they did. Besides, I want those two freezers."

"We haven't a freezer on the premises," Mr. Hatfield said again.

Wearily, he told the caretaker what had happened.

"You're handing me a line about not knowing where those freezers came from," Old Terry

Strawberry Ice Cream

growled. "For that matter, how do I know they aren't here somewhere?"

"You may look around, if you like," Mr. Hatfield invited.

"Thanks, I'll do that," he replied.

Old Terry inspected the clubroom and then to the deepening annoyance of the Cubs and their parents, went down into the basement. Finally, he seemed satisfied that the missing freezers were not in the building.

"Mr. Treuhaft, won't you have some cake and a dish of store ice cream?" Midge's mother invited graciously.

"No, Ma'am, I won't," he declined the invitation. "I'm leaving now."

He stomped out, allowing the door to bang behind him.

"Good riddance," Red exclaimed.

The Cubs began to straighten the clubroom, preparatory to leaving. Everyone was tired and a little discouraged even though the party had been a success.

"Old Terry spoiled everything," Dan said, expressing the sentiment of his Cubmates. "Do you suppose he could have been right?"

"About those stolen freezers belonging to the Christian Church?" Mr. Hatfield inquired.

"That's what I was thinking."

"I have a hunch they were the same ones, Dan."

"Then we actually were using stolen freezers?"

"I'm afraid of it, Dan. Someone played a joke on us. Not a very nice joke either."

"Then we're guilty of what they said!"

"We're not guilty of anything, Dan. If those freezers were taken from the church and delivered here, how were we to know who brought them or why? We accepted the gift in good faith."

"The trustees will have a better case than ever against us now."

"They may try to make something of the incident. However, I don't propose to worry about it."

"Think how much worse it would have been for us, if Old Terry actually had found the freezers," Brad chuckled. "As it is, he has no evidence."

"That's so," Dan agreed relaxing. "Whoever swiped the ice cream, did us a small favor. I only wish I knew for sure whether or not Pat had a finger in the deal."

Strawberry Ice Cream

"Given a little time, we may learn that too," Mr. Hatfield replied, smiling.

Though the Cubs pressed him for an explanation, the Cub leader would not reveal what was in his mind.

"Wait and we'll see," he suggested. "And while you're waiting, don't forget to practice hard at basketball. It's more important than ever now, that we prove to Pat and his boys that Cubs can win honorably!"

CHAPTER 10

OLD TERRY'S DEMAND

THE loss of the two ice cream freezers and the mystery surrounding them, distressed the Cubs. A dozen questions plagued their minds. Had someone stolen the freezers from the church and given them to the organization just to cause trouble?

Who had tipped Old Terry that the containers would be found at the Cub party? The Cubs kept mulling over the affair and the conviction grew upon them that Pat Oswald had been responsible.

"I wish we never had agreed to play the basketball series," Midge said gloomily one afternoon the following week when the boys were at the gymnasium. "We'll be the laughing stock of Webster City if we lose."

"Not if we lose fair and square," Dan returned, undisturbed. "It's no disgrace not to win. After all, it's only a game."

"Pat and his boys from Bay Shore way have all but ruined our reputations in this town!"

"The organization is under a cloud," Dan admitted.

Old Terry's Demand

The situation actually was more serious than he liked to acknowledge. Since the night of the party, word had spread throughout Webster City that Old Terry had caught the Cubs with property stolen from the Christian Church basement.

Friends and acquaintances of the Den 2 boys knew that the tale was untrue. Whenever the Cubs encountered others repeating the story, they denied it vigorously. How well their assertions were believed, they could not tell.

Never by word nor act had Mr. Hatfield even hinted that he doubted the Cubs. Repeatedly he assured them that the truth would come out in the end. Yet, sometimes the Cub leader looked so worried, the boys wondered if he weren't keeping really bad news from them.

Since the night of the party, Dan had seen Pat Oswald only once. The Bay Shore boy had come to the Cub clubroom to ask if the Purple Five might have a final practice in the gymnasium before the Friday night game.

"I suppose so," Dan had told him. "You'll have to talk to Mr. Hatfield about it."

Pat had loitered too long to please the Cubs. Deliberately, he looked over the exhibits, the achievement lists, and especially Fred's fort.

"Heard your party was a bust the other night," he twitted Dan. "Someone stole your ice cream, eh?"

"It was a low down trick." Dan looked the Bay Shore boy squarely in the eyes and Pat's gaze wavered. "You wouldn't know anything about it, would you?"

"Who, me? What an idea!" Pat laughed uproariously.

He slipped out the clubroom door before Dan could fire any more questions at him.

The Bay Shore boys practiced the following night at the gymnasium. Brad, who witnessed the workout, reported to the Cubs that the team had improved considerably.

"That Friday game will be no push-over for the Cubs," he warned. "Dig in!"

The Cubs spent every spare hour at the gymnasium, practicing baskets and working out their team plays. Both Dan and Midge were certain of final selection as forwards. Red and Chips too were improving daily in their ability to guard. Brad, at center, though he did less practicing than the others, was the surest of all the players at handling the ball.

It was Chub who gave the Cubs concern. The

Old Terry's Demand

youngster tried hard enough, but his fingers seemed coated with grease. Even if he received an easy, straight pass, he missed as often as he caught the ball.

"We'll have to use Chub as a substitute," Brad told his teammates. "The only thing is, what if one of the regulars can't play? Or if he goes out on a foul?"

"Pat's team is short a good substitute too," Dan declared. "No use borrowing trouble."

He was bouncing the ball lazily down the floor, when the gymnasium door burst open. Midge and Red rushed breathlessly in, fairly bursting with news.

"Come on outside, quick!" Red commanded. "Want to show you something!"

Dan, Brad and Chips quickly joined the other two Cubs at the rear church steps. There stood the two ice cream freezers, the lid missing from one of the cans!

"Gosh!" Chips exclaimed, staring. "Where'd they come from?"

"Midge and I just brought 'em from the river."

"The river?" echoed Dan. "I don't get it."

"Midge and I were hiking out that way," Red

explained. "All at once, we came upon these two cans."

"How did they get there?"

"Someone carried 'em, that's what," Red went on grimly. "Pat and his gang, I'll bet. The kids from Bay Shore play along the river a lot. They've made a stick and grass hut down by the Hi-Level Bridge."

"It was near the hut that we found the freezers," Midge added.

The Cubs were relieved to recover the missing containers, but uncertain what to do with them. One of the freezers seemed as good as new after they had washed out the metal cylinder which bore traces of melted ice cream. The other can was bent and the lid missing.

"We looked everywhere in the brush for it," Midge reported. "Couldn't find it anywhere."

Brad told the Cubs that not a moment must be lost in returning the stolen property to Terry Treuhaft.

"All we can do is try to explain to him again what happened, and offer to pay for the damaged freezer," he advised.

"We'll have to return 'em," Dan agreed uneasily.

Old Terry's Demand

"I hate to do it though. This will give him another chance to accuse us."

No one wanted to be assigned the job of returning the recovered property to Mr. Treuhaft. Because the other Cubs were so reluctant, Dan and Brad volunteered.

Both freezers were loaded into Dan's little red wagon, and made a tight fit. As the two boys hauled the containers down the street, they imagined that everyone was staring at them.

"I think half the town heard that untrue story about us taking these freezers," Dan said uncomfortably. "Now folks will think the worst, seeing us haul them."

"We've done nothing dishonorable, Dan."

"I know that, Brad. All the same, I feel sort of funny. Everyone stares so."

"We could go down this alley," Brad suggested, halting the wagon at the entranceway.

"Let's," agreed Dan.

They turned into the narrow alley, pulling the creaking wagon down the uneven bricks, past high fences and garbage cans.

Unaccountably, Brad halted so suddenly that the freezers nearly tumbled off the wagon.

Dan Carter and the Cub Honor

"See what I see, Dan?"

Near the exit to the alley, a group of boys were practicing basketball.

A make-shift netting had been attached to the wall, serving as a basket.

"Why, it's Pat Oswald!" Dan recognized one of the players. "No wonder he has a sure eye for a basket."

"I'm not blaming him for practicing," Brad commented in a low tone. "More power to him! But it's tough to have to do it in an alley."

"Pat didn't tell us about not having a practice court." Dan now felt ashamed of himself for having resented, even secretly, the Purple Five's use of the church gymnasium.

Not wishing to appear to spy upon the Bay Shore boys, Brad and Dan would have retreated. But as they started to turn the wagon, its squeaking wheels betrayed them.

"Hey, you!" Pat shouted, recognizing them.

Brad and Dan then went on, well aware that the freezers they hauled would create a sensation.

"Where'd you get those?" Pat demanded suspiciously.

Old Terry's Demand

Dan brought the wagon to a stop by the high fence.

"Down by the river," he replied briefly. "Some of the Cubs found them near your hut."

"Our hut? That's a laugh! You tryin' to say we took your old ice cream last Friday night?"

"I'm not making any accusations."

"Well, you'd better not, that's all I got to say!" Pat retorted. He glared at Dan, and then turned to his cronies. "Come on, guys! Let's scram! You can't have any privacy these days, not even in an alley."

Dan and Brad watched in amusement as the Bay Shore boys clattered noisily off over the uneven bricks. The thrust about finding the freezers near the gang's hut had found its mark, they felt.

"Pat looked guilty when he saw these cans," Brad remarked. "It burns me he'd engineer such a mean trick, especially after the Cubs have been mighty nice about the gymnasium."

Dan had been studying the make-shift basket netting fastened to the wall. A white chalk line, evidently a foul line marker had been drawn on the alley floor.

"Pat and his boys must practice here often," he remarked.

"I'd judge so, by the looks of the wall!" In annoyance, Brad pointed to a phrase which had been chalked on the boards.

The wording read: "The Cubs Are Sissies!" And higher up appeared the insult: "Cubs are Crooks!"

Dan dropped the wagon tongue and rushed over to wipe the offending words from the wall.

"This is the limit!" he fumed. "Brad, let's call off that Friday game! Why should we play with such wretched sports?"

"I know how you feel, Dan," Brad answered soothingly. "Pat acts like a baby. He wants to get our goat."

"He's had mine for a long while."

"We can't very well call off the game," Brad said slowly. "Mr. Hatfield talked it over with me only yesterday. He's heartsick at the way Pat has been acting, but he thinks we should go ahead and set the Bay View boys an example."

"I'd rather punch 'em in the nose."

"Take it easy, Dan."

"Oh, I'll control myself," Dan grinned. "Anyway, I want to lick 'em in that Friday game."

"That may not be so easy."

As Brad spoke, his gaze suddenly came to focus

Old Terry's Demand

upon knife scratchings on the board wall directly behind the other boy. Without saying more, he went over to inspect the deep cuts.

"Another insult to the Cubs, I suppose," Dan remarked.

Brad's broad shoulders blocked his view so that he could not see what it was that the Den Chief examined with such intent interest.

"This is something else, Dan," Brad said, finally moving aside.

On the wall, freshly cut with a sharp knife, were the carved initials: "P. O."

"Pat Oswald," Dan identified them. "Seems to me we've seen those same initials before, Brad. I guess we know now, who wrecked the old church building!"

CHAPTER 11

THE LOCKED DOOR

DISCOVERY of the carved initials on the alley wall convinced both Dan and Brad that the mutilation had been done by Pat Oswald.

The Bay Shore boy, they were sure, had a careless habit of using his jack-knife whenever he felt like it.

"These letters 'P. O.' are made the same as the ones we saw in the old church," Brad declared, studying the knife cuts closely. "At least I think so. I wish we could compare them."

"Is this enough evidence to convict Pat?"

"I'm afraid not, Dan. In the first place, being convinced of a thing is a lot different than being able to prove it. We didn't see Pat carve these initials, nor those on the church pew."

Dan lost interest in the wall markings. "What's the use then?" he asked hopelessly. "We'll never be able to prove anything."

"Oh, I don't know. I have a hunch Pat will overplay his hand. He's so cocky and sure of himself. Given time he may trip himself up."

The Locked Door

"Maybe, but I doubt it. You know as well as I do, that he and his bunch swiped our ice cream, but will we ever be able to prove that either?"

"We may. It takes time, Dan. You're too impatient."

"I just hope things turn out the way you predict, Brad. Somehow I've got an uneasy feeling about that game Friday night. You sure we shouldn't cancel it?"

"With at least a hundred tickets sold?"

"I guess not," Dan admitted. He sighed and started with the wagon and the ice cream freezers on down the deserted alley.

The scheduled basketball game between the two teams had attracted an unusual amount of interest in Webster City. Not only had the parents and friends of the Cubs bought tickets at twenty-five cents each, but a surprising number had been sold to strangers and friends of Pat Oswald and his group.

Though the Cubs had not really expected that the ticket sale would bring in very much, they now realized that it would swell their treasury considerably. The money already was earmarked for the payment of attorney fees, if needed.

After a long, tiring haul, the two Cubs eventually arrived with the freezers at Terry Treuhaft's cottage. The yard was choked with unraked leaves and the garage doors were locked.

"No one at home," Dan observed. "Just our luck!"

After rapping several times without an answer, the boys debated what to do. Brad was opposed to hauling the freezers back to the clubroom.

"We could leave them here," he suggested.

"Wouldn't it be better to take them back to the church? That's where they belong."

"All right," Brad agreed. "After we get home, I'll telephone Terry or one of the trustees so they'll know we returned them."

The old Christian churchyard looked more forlorn than ever as the boys presently came up to it with their creaking wagon. The lawn was deep with crackling brown leaves which filled their shoes with a fine dust.

"Say, we could build a dandy fort here," Dan remarked.

"And get run off the premises again! Nothing doing."

Dan grinned goodnaturedly, for the idea had not been a serious one. He was as eager as Brad to be

The Locked Door

rid of the ice cream freezers and be on his way home.

"Where'll we leave 'em?" he asked. "Not out front."

"No, they'll be safer around back."

The boys circled the church, finally halting by a rear door which led down into the basement.

"Why, it's open!" Dan exclaimed.

Someone had left the door unlocked, for it stood an inch or two ajar.

"Maybe Terry is here, or one of the trustees, Dan!"

Cautiously, the Cubs opened the door wider. They could see no one in the dark hallway. Nor could they hear anyone moving about inside the old church.

"Anyone here?" Brad finally shouted.

His voice echoed faintly, but there was no other sound.

"Queer," the Den Chief muttered. "The church is empty. But this door shouldn't have been unlocked. No wonder so much damage was done here. Terry isn't as careful about looking after the place as he'd have the trustees believe."

"So long's the door is unlocked, why not take the

freezers down into the basement where they belong?"

"We-ll," Brad hesitated. "Think we should?"

"It will only take a jiffy. They'll be a lot safer there than sitting outside where anyone coming along could grab 'em."

"Okay," Brad consented. "Let's be quick about it though. I'd hate to have Terry or one of the trustees catch us here. Then they'd really have a complaint."

With dispatch, the Cubs unloaded the first freezer and carried it between them to the cellar. The main furnace room was damp and musty. A rat scurried past, nearly brushing Dan's leg.

"Whoops!" he exclaimed, shivering. "I don't like this dark old hole, Brad."

"Weren't you the one who wanted to bring the freezers down here?" Brad reminded him with a chuckle. "That old rat won't hurt you. He was more scared than you are."

"Who says I'm scared? It just startled me, that's all."

The boys carried the freezer into the fruit closet. Nearly all of the long shelves which lined the wall were empty. A few cans of homemade fruit, evi-

The Locked Door

dently abandoned when the church was closed, remained. Dan noticed that a can of peaches and one of strawberries had been broken open.

"Come on, let's get that other freezer and be out of here," Brad urged. "No time to start looking around."

In haste, they went upstairs again to fetch the second container. Brad breathed a relieved sigh when it was safely on the shelf.

"That's done," he declared. "I'd hate—"

"You'd hate what?" Dan demanded as the other suddenly broke off.

"Nothing. Let's get out of here."

Dan knew from Brad's odd manner that something had startled him. As for himself, he had heard no unusual sound.

"What was it?" he demanded, dropping his voice to a half-whisper.

"Don't start whispering or you'll give me the jitters," Brad scolded.

"You did hear something?"

"Just the creaking of a board." Brad forced himself to be indifferent. "But what of it? This building has been closed up for a long while and the wood is dry. It wasn't anything."

"Let's go," Dan urged, leading the way up the dark stairs.

Though he wouldn't have admitted it, he too felt suddenly uneasy. In a way, it had been foolish of them to enter the empty building. If someone should find them there, it might be all but impossible to convince anyone of their true purpose.

The Cubs relaxed a bit as they reached the top of the basement stairs. Their fear of not being alone in the building began to ebb.

"Say, while we're here, I might take another quick look at those initials that were carved on the church bench," Brad proposed. "I'll probably never get another chance like this."

"Okay," Dan agreed reluctantly. "But make it snappy."

While Brad went into the main part of the church, the denner remained in the vestibule. He caught himself shivering. Nervousness? Or was it the chill wind which came in occasional drafts down the circular iron stairway leading to the belfry?

"I wish Brad would hurry," Dan kept thinking.

He was annoyed by his own uneasiness. What was it about this old church building that always gave him the same uncomfortable feeling? Why

The Locked Door

did he have that vague sensation—a sort of conviction that someone was watching him? Every crack and cranny of the vestibule seemed to have leering eyes.

Dan began to think of the first day he had visited the place. Chub too had been uneasy. Even then there had been strange sounds, a tapping bell, a shadowy figure in the church graveyard. And why had the church door been left unlocked?

A slight noise which he could not immediately localize, caused Dan to stiffen. Had the sound come from the belfry room? A bat, perhaps.

Dan listened intently. Distinctly, he could hear tiptoeing steps on the iron stairway! Someone was up there, stealthily descending!

Panic momentarily overcame the boy. "Brad!" he yelled. "Brad!"

It was reasuring to hear the older Cub yell: "Coming!"

"What's wrong?" Brad demanded, popping into the vestibule. "You look as if you'd seen a ghost."

"I didn't see anything, but I have a bad case of the jitters," Dan admitted sheepishly.

"It's time we quit this place anyhow," Brad replied. "I'm sure those carved initials on the pew are the same as the ones we saw in the alley. Pat Oswald must have carved them both."

Dan nodded scarcely listening. He cast an uneasy glance toward the iron stairway.

"Say, what's wrong with you anyhow?" Brad demanded.

Dan was ashamed to tell him of his fears. Now that Brad was with him again, he didn't feel as nervous as before. Like as not he'd allowed his imagination to play tricks on him again.

"Nothing's wrong," he muttered. "Let's go."

They left the vestibule. Dan reached for the knob of the rear, outside door. When he twisted it, an empty feeling came into his stomach. He tugged, but the door refused to budge.

"Stuck?" Brad asked, moving close.

Dan's lips had drawn into a tight, white line. "Not stuck," he managed in a faint voice, "Locked!"

CHAPTER 12

RULES OF BASKETBALL

"LOCKED?" Brad repeated, stunned by Dan's disclosure. "Why, it couldn't be."

He went quickly to the door to test it for himself.

"We're trapped in here," Dan gasped, truly unnerved. "Someone must have come along and locked us in. What'll we do?"

"Take it cool, for one thing," Brad replied, forcing himself to remain very calm. "Hey, look here!"

He pointed to the bolt which had been shot into place from the inside of the building.

"Well, what d'you know?" Dan mumbled.

"In your excitement, you must have locked that door yourself."

"I never did!" Dan denied. "I haven't been near this door since we came in and toted the freezers downstairs."

"Then how'd it get locked from the inside? I know I didn't do it."

As the full realization of what could have happened, dawned upon the two, they stared at each other an instant. Neither voiced the thought that someone might be in the building with them, but Dan involuntarily raised his eyes toward the darkening belfry steps. Those creaking sounds he had heard now seemed to have significance.

"Let's see if we can get out of here," Brad said gruffly.

The bolt stuck. He struck it sharply with his fist, and it flew back. The door opened readily.

"That's a relief!" Dan exclaimed, drawing a natural breath again. "And how!"

The two cubs hurriedly left the building. Having no key, they could not lock the church door from the outside.

"Anyway, we're leaving it just as we found it, Brad said. "Dan, you're sure you didn't slip that bolt in an absent-minded moment?"

"Positive."

"So am I." Brad frowned thoughtfully. "It must have been done while we were in the cellar. But who did it?"

"And what became of the person who locked us in?" Dan demanded in a hushed voice. "Do you suppose—?"

"He, she or IT is still in there?" Brad finished the sentence.

Rules of Basketball

"You have to admit it's sort of spooky."

"It's disturbing all right," Brad agreed. "Maybe we were locked in by accident. But if so, someone had to be in that church. And that someone must be still there."

The Cubs gazed reflectively at the old building. Despite their suspicion that it might have an occupant, nothing could have induced them to return for an inspection.

"Maybe it was Terry," Brad said doubtfully. "He could have heard us inside, and played a joke."

Dan shook his head. "It wasn't Terry, I'm sure, Brad. If he had caught us there, he would have raised cain."

"I think so myself."

Dan indicated the little red wagon which had been used to haul the freezers. He pointed out that anyone approaching the old church certainly would have seen it and know of their presence inside the building.

"Someone did it to scare us away, Brad." he declared. "I didn't tell you, but I was sure I heard footsteps on the stairway leading to the belfry."

"You think someone may have been hiding there, Dan?"

"I'm wondering."

Dan Carter and the Cub Honor

"Not one of Pat's gang, I hope."

"This old church is awfully close to the river and the railroad tracks," Dan remarked. "Someone could be using the place without the trustees knowing. I suspect Old Terry isn't as careful about keeping windows and doors locked as he's supposed to be."

"We could go back inside and check—"

"Not now, anyway," Dan said quickly. "We're in enough hot water as it is."

Brad agreed with the denner that it would be unwise to investigate further that day. He proposed, however, that they inform Mr. Hatfield of their findings, and also Terry Treuhaft.

The very next day, Dan ran into the old caretaker on a downtown street. Drawing him into conversation, he told of finding the unlocked door.

"How'd it get unlocked?" Terry demanded. "I never left it that way."

The caretaker was not as angry about the Cubs returning the ice cream freezers as Dan had expected him to be. Encouraged, he even dared reveal that the lid to one of the containers was missing.

"Yeah?" Old Terry grunted. "I reckon it can't be helped. Anyhow, those freezers ain't been used in years."

Rules of Basketball

Dan gazed at the caretaker in sheer amazement, wondering if he were ill. Why this sudden change of heart toward the Cubs?

"Thanks for the tip about the door," Terry said. "I'll check up on it right away." He started off, then paused and said awkwardly: "About that suit the trustees are threatening to bring—"

"Yes?"

"Just wanted you to know, I kinda changed my ideas about the Cubs."

"Then you realize we had nothing to do with wrecking that building or taking the freezers?"

"I been checkin' around," the caretaker admitted. "Folks everywhere have a good word for the Cubs."

"I wish you could convince the trustees they should drop their action."

"That won't be so easy, Dan," Terry sighed. "Mr. Maxwell is a determined man. I'll put in a good word though for the Cubs."

"Thanks," Dan said gratefully. "Thanks a lot."

The next few days he waited expectantly, hoping that very good news would come of his talk with Terry. When nothing happened, he and the other Cubs became discouraged again. From Mr. Hatfield they learned that apparently there had been no

Dan Carter and the Cub Honor

change in the attitude of the church trustees.

"Seemingly, they intend to go ahead with their court action," the Cub leader informed the boys. "We'll have to hire ourselves a lawyer."

Advance ticket sale for the Friday night basketball had been very large. On the evening of the game, the gymnasium was packed.

"Say, I'll bet we've taken in twenty or thirty dollars at least!" Fred Hatfield excitedly reported to the other Cubs. "This will be a big boost for our treasury."

Game time was at seven o'clock. Shortly before the hour, Pat Oswald and his four players trotted out on the floor to practice a few baskets.

"Get a load of those suits!" Chips muttered to Dan.

The five players wore new, bright-hued purple sport shirts. By contrast, the Cubs had nondescript shorts and shirts, no two alike.

"And look at that guy shoot baskets," Chips went on gloomily. "He can't miss!"

He nodded his head toward Pat, who was winning applause from the crowd by his dead-aim at the basket.

"Just get in there and guard him," Dan urged.

Rules of Basketball

"Don't let him get a chance to throw."

The game began with one of the high school teachers, Jim Veeley, acting as referee.

Midge and Dan played as forwards, Chips guarded Pat Oswald, and Red was assigned to another bulky player. Fred and Chub sat on the sidelines as substitutes.

Brad, several inches shorter than his opponent at center, missed the toss-up. The Purple Five gained possession of the ball. Back and forth they passed it, jeering at the Cubs. Then they fed it to Pat.

Before Chips could come awake, the Purple Five forward brushed roughly past him. Quick as a cat, he dribbled directly under the basket, and hooked an easy one through the netting.

The Purple Five had scored in the first minute of play!

A ripple of applause came from the audience for the basket had been a pretty one. On the south side of the gymnasium where rooters for the Bay Shore boys had congregated, loud cheering broke out.

"Get in there, Cubs!" rooters for Den 2 called. "Come on!"

The Cubs were on their toes now, determined not to let the Purple Five score again. But they couldn't seem to get their hands on the ball.

Pat was a one-man team, darting here, there everywhere. Poor Chips was winded trying to keep up with the fleet-footed forward. Repeatedly, the Purple Five scored, while Dan managed only one basket.

As the Purple Five's score climbed, Pat became even more flashy and bold. He'd shove Chips aside to snatch the ball, and twice he jabbed him with his elbow. Twice the referee warned him for roughness. Then he called a personal foul.

A howl of indignation went up from the section of Bay Shore rooters.

"Served Pat right!" Chips muttered. "He's been getting by with murder."

He took his place on the freethrow line, waited for the noise to subside, and tossed the ball. It went through the netting, tallying a point for the Cubs.

After that, two other fouls were called in rapid succession on Pat. In each instance, the Cubs scored on the freethrow.

When the half finally ended, the score stood 10 to 5 in favor of the Purple Five.

As the boys rested, Mr. Veeley came around to speak to Pat.

Rules of Basketball

"One more foul and you'll be out of the game," he warned. "Better watch it next half."

The game began again and Pat observed the rules more carefully. But now, instead of trying repeatedly for the ball, he would bounce it lazily back and forth among his teammates. Clearly, the Bay Shore boys meant to play a delaying game.

"Break it up! Break it up!" shouted the rooters.

The Cubs tried their best. Seeing the ball coming toward him on a straight pass, Dan reached for it.

At that instant, Pat darted in, striking the Cub's arm just as his fingers would have closed upon the ball.

A howl of anger arose from the crowd. Mr. Veeley held up his hands in signal of another personal fowl on Pat.

Dan made the free throw. Pat was ordered off the floor.

"You can't do that," he protested. "We don't have any regular substitute."

His arguments were unavailing. Pat finally left the floor, muttering to himself. A lean, lanky substitute took his place.

After that, it was a losing game for the Purple Five. With Pat on the sidelines, the team collapsed.

The Cubs brought the score even, and then Dan dropped three baskets in succession to win the game by a six point margin.

"Well, we won, boy!" Brad declared as they trotted off the floor after the final whistle had blown. "You were great, Dan!"

"We didnt' have too much competition after Pat went out of the game," Dan replied, brushing dirt from his shorts. "I wish we could have won with him opposing us."

"It was his own fault," Brad shrugged. "Mr. Veeley warned him."

The Purple Five and their rooters took defeat with poor grace. There were mutterings of "We were robbed!" and remarks that the referee had been unfair.

"Maybe you want to call off the other two games," Brad suggested quietly to Pat.

"No such thing," the other boy retorted. "Next time we'll lick you so you'll never forget it. Besides, we need the cash."

"What d'you mean?" Brad demanded, already guessing the answer.

"The gate," Pat explained with an impudent grin. "You Cubs took in a lot of dough tonight. Well, we want our share. Half of it belongs to us."

CHAPTER 13

HALLOWEEN PRANKS

WORD spread around the gymnasium of Pat's outrageous demand. Brad and Dan brought Mr. Hatfield, fully expecting him to reject the request.

"Pat, you feel you should have half the money?" the Cub leader questioned him.

"Sure." The captain of the Purple Five eyed the group of Cubs defiantly. However, his gaze wavered under the level scrutiny of Mr. Hatfield. "We earned it, didn't we? What's more, we'd have won the game, if we hadn't been cheated."

"Cubs do not cheat," Mr. Hatfield replied. "When you know more about the organization, you'll understand that. We play according to the rules, that's all."

"You make 'em to suit yourselves," Pat growled.

"On the contrary, you'll find them all printed in the official rule book on basketball. It might be well for your team to study up a bit before the next scheduled game."

"We'll study all right! Now, how about the dough? You're holding out, I take it?"

"If you feel you're entitled to a share, you may have it," Mr. Hatfield said. He turned to Dan, saying: "Go bring Mr. Holloway. He has all the money we collected tonight."

Dan's jaw dropped, but he obeyed the order without question. What had come over the Cub leader anyhow? Pat and the Bay Shore boys certainly hadn't done anything to earn any of the money! Why, the Cubs had sold nearly all of the tickets. Besides, the organization would be expected to pay the church a smal fee for use of the gymnasium to cover lights and heating. It was unfair!

Mr. Holloway came quickly, carrying a box in which were the receipts. He reported to the Cub leader that the correct total was $30.80.

"Pat here demands half as his share," Mr. Hatfield said. "I've told him that he may have it. The Cubs make a point of being honest. We'd rather lose the entire amount than to take one penny that doesn't belong to us."

Pat's cheeks flamed, but he continued to grin in a silly, arrogant sort of way.

Mr. Holloway counted out exactly $15.40 which he poured into the boy's hands. "Sure it's enough?" he asked.

"We'll make it do."

Halloween Pranks

As he pocketed the cash, Pat's gaze again swept the group of Cubs. Though no one spoke, their silence made him fully aware of their contempt. He hesitated and for just an instant, Dan thought he intended to return the money. Then, with a shrug, Pat was gone.

Once his footsteps had died away, the Cubs gave vent to their anger. Mr. Hatfield allowed them to have their say without comment. He did not try to explain his action in giving the money to Pat. His only remark was: "I'm trying a little experiment, boys. Let's wait and see."

While the talk was at his height, Fred came rushing into the gymnasium.

"Hey, come quick!" he urged.

"What's wrong?" Brad demanded. "Anyone hurt?"

"Come on and I'll show you," Fred answered, motioning for the boys to follow him upstairs to the clubroom. "I'm so mad I could chew nails!"

The Cubs, followed by Mr. Hatfield and Mr. Holloway, hastened up the stairway. Fred dramatically flung open the clubroom door.

"Just look!" he exclaimed. "This must have been done only a few minutes ago."

Dan Carter and the Cub Honor

The cardboard fort which had been built with such painstaking care, lay demolished on the floor.

"All my work—gone!" Fred said.

No one spoke for a moment. Everyone felt sick at heart. All the Cubs had been proud of the fort and knew that Fred had spent hours of time completing it.

"This was wrecked right after the game," Fred said bitterly.

"How do you place the time?" Mr. Hatfield's voice was quiet though troubled.

"I dropped in here for a minute between halves of the game. The fort was okay then. When I came upstairs just a bit ago, this was what I found!"

"Pat or some of his gang did it," Chips announced with finality. "That's all the thanks we get for giving 'em half the money."

"I didn't think they'd do a trick like this," Mr. Hatfield said. "I'd hoped—well, I thought Pat had good stuff in him buried deep down in. Seems I was mistaken."

"We ought to report this to the police," Red said indignantly. "Want me to call 'em?"

"No, Red. This is hardly a case for the police."

Halloween Pranks

"How about those other two basketball games?" Midge asked. "Will we play them?"

"That I think, is for the Cubs to decide. After what happened tonight, I'm sure we'd be justified in cancelling."

"Only trouble is that if we do, they'll go around Webster City calling us yellow," Brad said. He began picking up the scattered sections of the destroyed fort. "I say, let's play the series, and lick 'em."

The debate waxed warm for a few minutes. Finally, however, a majority of the Cubs voted in favor of carrying on the series.

"Very well, if that's the decision," Mr. Hatfield said. "One thing, though! The game must not be used as a means of venting spite on the Bay Shore boys. If we play them, we must conduct ourselves as good sports. Agreed?"

The next game had been scheduled for the following Friday. With Pat and his players claiming half the receipts, the Cubs had far less enthusiasm for selling tickets during the week. Nevertheless, news had traveled that the game would be a good one. Accordingly, many persons stopped the Cubs on the street to ask for the tickets.

The Cubs were not surprised to learn that Pat had told around that the Purple Five had been cheated out of victory on a technicality.

"They'll be laying for us next game," Brad warned the boys of Den 2 one night as they practiced at the church gymnasium. "If we want to win, we've got to improve our teamwork."

The Cubs had worked out several new plays which seemed to go fairly well. Chub however, could not get the hang of them. The others noticed that his mind never seemed entirely on the game. A ball would be tossed in his direction, and he'd seem aware of it only after it had shot past him.

"Chub, you've got to wake up!" Brad scolded him.

"I—I'm sorry," Chub apologized.

He'd try harder for awhile, and then his mind would wander again. The Cubs felt sorry for him because obviously he meant well. Chub though, was a total loss to the team, even as a substitute.

"Something's bothering Chub," Brad confided to Dan. "He's worrying about things, and he'll never be any good until he gets it off his chest. Any idea what's wrong?"

Halloween Pranks

"It may be because he hasn't any father or mother," Dan replied. "I've tried to talk to him now and then, but he never opens up."

The next few days were so delightful that the Cubs abandoned basketball for hikes. They decorated their clubroom with cornstalks and pumpkins obtained from a nearby farm.

Fred made cardboard witches for the walls, and in the work forgot his disappointment over loss of the cardboard fort.

All the Cubs fashioned Halloween costumes and laid plans for another party. They took care however, that Pat and his cronies should not learn of the affair.

Regularly, on Tuesdays and Thursdays, the Purple Five practiced thirty minutes in the church gymnasium. The Bay Shore area boys now were much better behaved and quieter while in the building.

Nevertheless, the Cubs could not forget past actions. By agreement no mention was made of the destroyed cardboard fort. The conviction remained however, that Pat and his gang were responsible for it as well as the damage to the old Christian

Church. Nor had they forgotten the ice cream freezer episode or Pat's unfair demand for half of the game receipts.

The Bay Shore boys were treated politely, but none of the Cubs warmed to them. Furthermore, while the Purple Five team was in the building, the clubroom always was kept locked.

"You guys don't trust us much, do you?" Pat demanded of Dan one afternoon on the final practice session before the coming Friday game.

"I wouldn't say that," Dan avoided the issue.

"Then why do you lock the clubroom? So we can't look in?"

"Our cardboard fort was wrecked, Pat. Fred had worked weeks on it. We don't want anything like that to happen again."

Pat bristled, and color flamed into his cheeks. "You think we did it?"

"I didn't say so, did I?"

"No, but you're acting mighty suspicious. I'm tired of being treated as if we have to be watched all the time. Believe me, if we wanted to do mischief, we could tear this place apart! But we got other plans for Halloween. Not a silly party either."

Pat's boastful manner instantly convinced Dan

Halloween Pranks

that the Purple Five team was planning mischief, come October 31. He asked a few casual questions, hoping to draw the other boys out.

"You'd like to know, wouldn't you?" Pat teased. He looped a ball through the basket, and called to his teammates. "Come on, guys! Let's move out of here! We got some important business to talk over."

Dan was disturbed by the hints the other had dropped. Undoubtedly, the Bay Shore boys intended to commit Halloween pranks. He only hoped the Cubs would not be blamed.

He heard no more of the matter and had nearly forgotten about it when Halloween finally came. The Den 2 boys had arranged a party at the Holloway home.

Everyone dressed in costume and the affair was a great success. Fred, as usual, won first prize, fixing himself up as an armored knight.

Dan wore an ordinary clown suit. The other Cubs came as ghosts or in over-sized clothes borrowed from their parents.

The party broke up at any early hour.

"No mischief tonight, boys," Mr. Hatfield warned as he dismissed the group. "But then, I know I can trust Cubs to behave themselves always."

Several of the Den 2 members were riding home with their parents. Dan and Brad had come alone. Mr. Hatfield offered to drive them home.

"No need to," Brad turned down the offer. "It's only a step. We don't mind walking."

"How about you, Chub?" the Cub leader inquired.

"We'll see him home," Dan volunteered. "It's not much out of our way."

Still wearing their costumes, the boys started away from the Holloway home. In this neighborhood, the streets were quiet. Some distance away, they could hear the tinkling of a cowbell.

"Nice night for the witches to howl!" Dan said jokingly.

"No pranks for us," Brad replied. "We're going home and to bed."

Enroute to Chub's home, the boys met two groups of masked children returning from parties. Lights blazed on residential porches, and a few small children were ringing doorbells, demanding: "Trick or Treat?"

"Kid stuff," Dan remarked. "I'm glad we're too old for that silliness."

Chub was left safely at his doorstep. Brad and

Halloween Pranks

Dan then turned off toward their own neighborhood. As they approached the old Christian Church, unconsciously they began to walk faster.

Suddenly, they were startled to hear a rush of footsteps in the direction of the old deserted building.

"What's that?" Brad demanded, halting to listen.

"Sounds like a gang of kids, running," Dan instantly decided. "Toward the church too! Golly, I hope—"

"The Cubs would be sunk if any more damage is done there," Brad finished for him.

"Let's find out what's happening."

"Okay, Dan. We'll have to move fast though."

Breaking into a run, the two headed directly for the church. As they approached from the front they could see no one on the grounds. A nearly full moon, rising through the bare branches of a scraggly tree, cast a soft, weird glow over the earth.

"I can't see anyone—" Brad began, only to break off.

The two listeners had heard a door slam. They were certain the sound had come from the rear of the old building.

Noiselessly, Brad and Dan moved around the

hedge to approach the church from the river side.

"Look!" Dan directed the other's attention.

A group of five or six boys clustered at the rear of the building, near an open coal chute. The sound which the Cubs had taken for the slamming of a door, had, in reality been the banging of the chute cover.

"It's Pat and his bunch!" Dan recognized them.

"Bent on trouble too! They're going into that building, and we'll get the blame."

As the pair crept cautiously nearer, they could hear Pat giving orders to his followers.

"I'll go first, he told them. "Then the rest of you follow. All but Pete, who's to stay here and keep watch. We'll get that bell from the belfry and dump it on main street!"

He disappeared feet first down the chute.

"The belfry bell!" Dan whispered in alarm. "This is the worst yet! If Pat gets by with it, the Cubs are almost sure to be blamed. What are we going to do, Brad? How can we stop 'em?"

CHAPTER 14

THE BELFRY BELL

BRAD could not provide a ready answer to Dan's demand for a means of stopping the Bay Shore boys in their Halloween prank.

The boy called Pete had been left on guard at the entrance to the coal chute. Pat and at least five others now were inside the empty building.

"We're two against six," Brad muttered. "We can't stop 'em, Dan."

"But to let them take the bell! The trustees are almost certain to blame the Cubs. If they'd only come here now and learn the truth!"

Brad had been thinking fast. "Our best bet is to telephone Mr. Hatfield and have him call the police," he whispered. "It will take 'em a few minutes to get that bell down. They aren't going to unfasten it half as easy as they think!"

"It will weigh a ton too! Say, maybe we will have time enough to nab 'em!"

"You dash for a 'phone, Dan," Brad advised in a

whisper. "Sneak around behind the hedge and don't let that kid, Pete, see you. I'll keep watch until you get back."

"I'll hurry as fast as I can."

Dan started to creep away. He had taken less than three steps when a sudden commotion inside the church brought him up sharply.

From the interior of the building, issued an eerie scream.

Then utter confusion! He could hear Pat and the other Bay Shore boys gasping and yelling as they evidently pushed and shoved one another down the iron stairway which led from the belfry.

Dan couldn't guess what had happened. Had one of the boys fallen on the stairs? But surely that wouldn't have been enough to have caused such panic.

As he hesitated, wondering whether to wait or hasten on to find a telephone, the intruders began to pour out of the building.

Pat was the first to crawl through the narrow opening.

"What happened?" Pete demanded. "Where's the bell?"

"Bell?" Pat laughed hysterically. "That bell can

The Belfry Bell

stay up there forever! The church is haunted!"

The other Bay Shore boys came out of the coal chute as fast as they could squeeze through. Without even waiting for their buddies, they started on a run away from the building.

Pat and Pete stayed until the last member of their gang had reached safety. Hastily, they slammed down the door of the coal chute.

At that moment, from overhead, came the faint tap-tap-tap of the church bell. It was a muted sound but one which could not have been caused by the light breeze which was blowing.

"Hear that?" Pat muttered fearfully. "I'm getting away from this place—fast!"

He fled, leaving Pete to bound after him. In another moment, Dan and Brad were the only two left in the churchyard.

"What d'you know?" Brad chuckled, recovering from the rapidity of the flight.

"We lost our chance to trap 'em inside the building," Dan said regretfully, returning to stand beside the Den Chief at the coal chute opening. "What do you suppose happened in there?"

"I wish I knew. Want to go inside and find out?"

"Say, are you kidding?"

Dan Carter and the Cub Honor

"Sure, I am," Brad chuckled. "You couldn't drag me into that building tonight. All the same, I'm mighty curious. Pat and his boys must have seen or heard something that completely unnerved them."

"Pat's no coward either."

"No, it would take plenty to jolt him, Dan. It was more than just a tapping bell." Brad gazed thoughtfully up at the dark belfry.

Dan shivered, feeling ill at ease. "That bell's enough to give me the jim-jams," he confessed. "This isn't the first time we're heard it. How do you explain it, Brad? You don't think the church could be—"

"Haunted? Say, be your age!"

"I know its' silly," Dan admitted, sheepishly. "But so many queer things have happened here."

"Man-made queer things."

"What do you mean by that, Brad?" Dan quickly caught him up.

The older boy, however, did not answer. He moved back a few paces so that he could obtain a better view of the shadowy belfry.

"See anything?" Dan asked, folowing him nervously.

"Nothing."

The Belfry Bell

"We didn't imagine the tapping of that bell, Brad."

"No, it sounded all right. And it didn't ring by itself either."

"Then you think someone may be up there—right now?"

"Could be."

"Gosh, it scares me to think about it," Dan muttered. "Even now, someone might be watching us, and we couldn't see him."

"Don't get yourself worked up," Brad advised in a matter-of-fact voice. "We're safe enough here so long as we don't go inside the building."

The boys circled the church, studying it from every angle. Now that Pat and the others had fled, it was difficult to believe that anything ever had been amiss. The old building appeared as deserted as on the day when the Cubs first had seen it.

"At any rate, we know how Pat and his bunch got inside the church that first time," Dan commented. "Through the coal chute."

Both he and Dan felt a trifle discouraged over the outcome of their little adventure. With half a break they might have caught the Bay Shore boys inside the building! Now, it seemed they were no closer than ever to proving the innocence of the Cubs.

"No use to telephone Mr. Hatfield now, or to call the police," Dan remarked, sunk in gloom. "We muffed it right, Brad."

"Oh, I wouldn't say so." The older boy was quite cheerful. We learned quite a bit. And we can be sure of one thing. I don't think Pat and his pals will come back here for awhile."

"Not after the way they poured out of that building." Dan grinned at the recollection. "I sure wish we could have had a picture! Even Pat was scared half out of his wits!"

"Hearing that bell tap gave me quite a start myself," Brad admitted frankly. "I wish I knew what it was that scared those kids. They must have seen something—not a ghost either!"

"Want to come back here sometime to investigate?" Dan proposed, half jokingly. "When it's daylight, I mean?"

"Maybe I will," the Den Chief replied. "I intend to talk this over with Mr. Hatfield. If he thinks we wouldn't run afoul of the trustees, I may try to get in there again to see what I can learn."

CHAPTER 15

MEASLES

HALLOWEEN was two days gone and no further investigation had been made of the old church by the river.

Brad had gone to Mr. Hatfield's home, fully intending to tell him of seeing Pat and his pals flee in panic from the building.

He never had been able to make his report. Mr. Hatfield, it developed, had been called out of the city on an important business trip. In his absence, Den 2 was under the direction of Mr. Holloway.

The Cub leader, Brad learned, expected to be back in Webster City in time for the Friday night basketball game with the Purple Five.

"We really shouldn't play that outfit, knowing what we do about 'em," the Den Chief confided to Dan. "Think we should tell the other Cubs what we know?"

"It wouldn't do any good, unless we cancel the game," Dan replied after thinking the matter over.

"Mr. Hatfield seemed to want us to treat Pat and his bunch with good will. So I suppose, if he were here, he'd advise us to go ahead with the game just as if nothing had happened."

"Then we won't say anything about the church affair," Brad decided. "It would only stir up bad feeling. The Cubs have it in for Pat as it is—and for good reasons too!"

Though the Den Chief had tried to keep his feelings from the younger boys, he was not too happy about the coming game. Pat and the Bay Shore boys smarted under the first defeat they had suffered from the Cubs. The second game in the series might be bitterly fought.

As for trying to pin evidence on Pat that he and his gang were responsible for the trouble at the Christian Church, he scarcely knew where to start. Any accusation he or Dan might make, would, of course, be denied.

"How about going out there again and trying to get in?" Dan proposed.

"Let's wait until Mr. Hatfield gets back," Brad turned him down. "With the accusation standing against us that we once broke into the place, we've

Measles

got to be cautious. If anyone should see us there, they might misunderstand."

So matters stood. Basketball practice went on each night after school. And outwardly at least, the Cubs were friendly with the Purple Five.

On the Friday set for the game, the Den 2 boys called a 15-minute practice session after school in the gymnasium.

"We're only going to shoot a few baskets and run through a couple of team plays," Brad instructed the group. "I want to be sure you fellows have it down pat. We'll run through Play B first. Chips, get in there, and start it off."

Chips, who slouched on a bench, moved sluggishly.

"You'll have to get more pep than that unless we want to be licked tonight," Brad said, passing him the ball. "Say, what's the matter with you anyhow?"

"I feel awful," Chips admitted in a weak voice. "Sort of sickish all over."

"Look at his face!" Dan directed.

Chips' cheeks and forehead were flushed. Even more alarming, the back of his neck was blotched with little red spots.

"I itch too," Chips said miserably.

The Cubs who had clustered about him, backed hastily away.

"O'my gosh," Brad groaned. "You're coming down with something, for sure. Get home as fast as you can, Chips, and into bed! Have your mother call a doctor."

"What about the game?"

"Let us worry about that. You beat it home."

Within an hour, the Cubs knew the worst. Chips had a mild case of the measles! He would be out of the game and confined to his home for more than a week.

The Cubs were too discouraged even to discuss the situation. Chub now would have to go into the game as a forward. That meant that Dan would be shifted to guard, given the task of trying to hold Pat to a minimum of baskets.

"We're sunk," he admitted privately to Brad as they laced their tennis shoes in the dressing room.

"Probably," the Den Chief agreed. "Let's do our best though. And if we're licked, let's take it like good sports."

An even larger crowd had gathered in the gymnasium than for the first game of the series. Fred jubilantly reported that despite a poor advance

Measles

ticket sale, thirty-seven dollars had been taken in at the door.

"One man paid a dollar," he told the Cubs. "Said he wanted to help with the organization's defense fund."

"And we have to give Pat and his chiselers half of the receipts!" Red remarked bitterly. "It's unfair!"

In glancing over the audience, Dan noticed many neighbors and other persons he knew. However, on the front row he observed a tall, thin man rather poorly dressed, whose face he did not recognize.

"Who is he?" Dan asked Brad, pointing out the stranger.

"No one I ever saw before. I don't think he was here last game."

"See how he keeps watching Chub," Dan directed the other's gaze. "I guess it must be because the kid's so unsure of himself."

"Chub does his best, Dan."

"Oh, I know that. I wasn't criticising him. It's not his fault he was thrust into this game."

The Cubs were convinced that without Chips to bolster their team, they would be whitewashed. However, each player was determined not to give up without a struggle.

Sharp at seven o'clock the whistle sounded and the game began. The Cubs were heartened by the arrival, albeit late, of Mr. Hatfield. Having come directly from a train, he still had his suitcase with him.

Both teams played cautiously at the start of the game. Pat and the other members of his team evidently were determined not to be tripped up on rules a second time.

To avoid personal fouls, the Purple Five boys quite outdid themselves. Once when Pat brushed hard against Dan as they both rushed for the ball, the Bay Shore boy actually muttered: "Excuse me, I didn't mean to hit you."

Surprisingly, with roughness eliminated, the Cubs held their own fairly well. Pat made two baskets, and then was unable to score as Dan kept hard on him.

Repeatedly, the Cubs had chances for baskets themselves. Team plays worked well, even without Chips. But Chub fumbled time after time at the critical moment. Once he shot and the ball hung on the rim, only to drop outside.

The half finally ended: 6 to 2 in favor of the Purple Five.

Measles

"If we only had you in there as forward, Dan," Brad said regretfully. "Chub tries, but he just can't find the basket."

During the second half, Fred was put in as a substitute for Chub. He and Midge, between them, managed three baskets. In the last quarter, Dan from far down the floor made a wild pass for the netting. The ball looped high and with a swishing sound, dropped cleanly through the mesh.

That brought the score: 6 to 6. Likewise, it aroused the Purple Five. Bearing down, they began to play roughly again. Foul after foul was chalked against the Bay Shore players. Each time, when a free throw was allowed, the Cubs failed to make the single point.

Pat had become chained lightning itself. He eluded Dan and time after time dropped the ball close, if not through the basket. When the final whistle blew, the score stood: 10 to 6 in favor of the Purple Five.

"I tried, but I couldn't hold Pat down," Dan confessed, as he sank down on a bench to catch his breath.

"You did fine, Dan," Mr. Hatfield said, throwing an arm around his shoulder. "I was proud of you.

Dan Carter and the Cub Honor

And of all the Cubs. Except for a few minutes toward the end, it was a good, clean game."

The Cubs hid their disappointment over loss of the game. They congratulated the Purple Five on the victory, and Dan made a point of speaking to Pat.

"You're just too good," he said with a grin. "It takes a better guard than Dan Carter to hold you."

Pat seemed surprised by the praise. "You were pretty fair yourself," he replied. "I missed a lot of baskets because of good guarding."

"Chips may be back for the third and deciding game of the series," Dan went on. "Now that both teams have a victory, that contest should be a honey."

Hot cocoa was being served the Cubs upstairs in the church dining room. Mr. Hatfield invited Pat and his teammates to join the other boys.

"Thanks," Pat answered, looking rather embarrassed. "I-I guess we won't. Next time, maybe."

"Then we'll count out your share of the receipts—"

"Skip it," Pat growled. He moved quickly away.

In leaving the gymnasium, Dan saw Chub talking

Measles

to the strange man who earlier had drawn his attention. As he came up, the two separated. Chub waited for him, his face troubled.

"Anything wrong, Chub?" Dan inquired.

Chub shook his head. "Only that I lost the game for the Cubs."

"No such thing," Dan said cheerfully. "Was it your fault Chips came down with the measles? Anyhow, I thought you played your very best game."

"Did you?" Chub brightened. "I tried awfully hard."

"Anything else bothering you?"

"Well, that man—he was asking me such funny questions."

"I noticed him during the game," Dan returned. "He paid a lot of attention to you."

"It gave me a queer feeling, talking to him."

"Queer? How so?"

Chub shrugged and could not explain. "He kept calling me Charles for one thing, just as if he knew me well. I never saw him before, but I had the strangest feeling as if I'd really known him a long while."

"Did he tell you his name?"

"No, but he asked me a dozen questions. He wanted to know where I lived, the school I attended —everything. The last question was the funniest of all. He said: "Chub, are you *happy* here in Webster City?"

"What did you tell him?"

"I didn't answer. You came up just then, and he went off."

"Don't let it bother you, Chub," Dan said. "The guy must have been a screw-ball."

"He was real nice, Dan. I—I liked him ever so much."

"Well, don't keep your mind on it," Dan said, linking arms with the boy and pulling him toward the stairway. "Come on, let's have some hot cocoa."

Chub went willingly enough. In fact, as they entered the dining room together, he failed to notice that the stranger still loitered in the outside vestibule.

Dan however, had seen him. He observed too that the man's gaze was following Chub's every move.

"Who can he be?" he speculated. "Why is he so interested in Chub?"

Dan gave himself a mental memo to try during

Measles

the next few days to learn more about the stranger. Meanwhile, why let it bother him? Following his advice to Chub, he brushed the matter entirely from his mind and joined the other Cubs at the cocoa table.

CHAPTER 16

THE STRANGER

IT was reassuring to learn that Chips had a very light case of measles. The Cubs, of course, were not permitted to see him. But Mrs. Davis reported to the den that her son could not be kept in bed and that his spots rapidly were disappearing.

Knowing that they all had been exposed to the disease, the Cubs kept their fingers crossed. Days passed however, and no other den member came down sick.

"Chips may be able to play in that last game with the Purple Five," Dan remarked one day as he and Brad walked to the public library together. "Think we have a chance to win?"

"With Chips, yes. We need him badly though."

"Chub never will make a good player that's for sure," Dan sighed. "I can't figure out that kid, Brad. He likes being a Cub, but somehow he doesn't catch on."

The Stranger

"Not at basketball," Brad admitted. "Something's bothering him. Say, come to think of it, he hasn't been at practice the last two nights."

"Maybe he's down with measles!"

"Never thought of that," Brad admitted. "We ought to find out."

The boys returned several books to the library and then decided to hike out to Chub's place to inquire.

In response to their rap on the door the Widow Lornsdale came to admit them. She assured them that Chub was quite well, though not at home just then.

"He may be off somewhere wandering in the woods," she added. "Poor lad! He seems so lonesome and unhappy."

"Doesn't he like being a Cub?" Dan inquired.

"Oh, indeed, he enjoys the organization very much. You know, though, that Chub's lot hasn't been an easy one."

Brad and Dan had no knowledge whatsoever of the boy's past. Remembering Mr. Hatfield's admonition not to ask questions, they never had tried to pry into his background.

"I've done what I could for Chub," the widow resumed. "He's a very good boy and deserves parents. Since Juvenile Court authorities placed him with me, I've had no trouble with him whatsoever."

Dan and Brad were startled by the reference to Juvenile Court. Was it posisble, they wondered, that Chub had at some time been a delinquent? It hardly seemed possible that anyone so shy and reserved could have given the authorities difficulty.

Thinking back, Dan recalled that the Juvenile Court director had spoken to Chub when the Cubs were touring the courthouse. Other referees there had seemed to know him too. Yet Chub never once had mentioned knowing any of the officials.

"Won't you boys come inside and wait?" the widow politely invited them. "I can't tell you when Chub will return though."

"Just tell him we were here," Brad directed. "We wanted to be sure he wasn't down with measles. Tell him we'll be counting on him for the game Friday night."

"I'll give him your message," the widow promised.

Dusk was coming on as Brad and Dan turned homeward. The old Christian Church, as usual, drew

The Stranger

them like a magnet. Though they might have chosen a shorter route, deliberately they selected the road which ran past the deserted building.

"We never did learn what scared Pat and his bunch Halloween night," Brad remarked, staring at the dark, unwinking windows.

"I tried to talk to him about it," Dan admitted. "He closed up like a clam."

Since that night when the two nearly had caught the Bay Shore boys in the building, Brad had discussed the matter only once with Mr. Hatfield. He never had given the Cub leader full information, for their conversation had been interrupted by the arrival of a third party.

"I sure wish I knew what it was that scared Pat half out of his wits," he remarked meditatively. "For half a cent—"

"You're not thinking of going in there?" Dan demanded.

"No-o, not now, anyway. I'd like to know, though, if the door to the coal chute still is unlocked. Anyone can get in and out of that building at will, and yet the Cubs are blamed for any damage done!"

Cutting across the church lawn, the two circled

around to the rear of the property. Brad checked the coal chute door.

"Still unlocked," he reported in disgust.

Dan had been trying the doors. One which opened into a rear corridor, swung inward at his touch.

"This is the limit!" he exploded. "Why any amount of damage could be done here! The place is wide open."

"Yet Terry puts out he's such a good caretaker! How those church trustees can claim to have any case against the Cubs is beyond me! It's queer though—"

"About the place being open? Old Terry locked the building up tight as a drum that first day he was here with the trustees. I saw him check the doors myself."

"Do you suppose someone else could have a key?" Brad speculated. "That is, someone besides the trustees?"

Dan did not answer. He stood peering in through the door he had shoved open. The old building was as quiet as a tomb.

"Brad—"

"Yeah?"

The Stranger

"This would be the perfect chance to make a last check of the place."

"We were in the building once, Dan."

"Not in the belfry. I'd like to find out what makes that bell tap so mysteriously. If we could learn the answer, it might clear up the case against the Cubs."

"And if we were caught, or even seen, what then?"

"That's a chance we'd have to take, Brad."

"I don't think Mr. Hatfield would like it," the Den chief said, deeply troubled. "I'm as curious as you are, but it's trespassing."

"The Cubs already are in the soup," Dan argued. "Unless we dig up some evidence that will help us, the trustees will carry out their threat to file suit."

"Yeah, you're right about that," Brad acknowledged. "If you want to wait here, I'll make a fast foray in to see what I can learn."

"Oh, no, you don't!" Dan retorted. "It was my idea, so I'm the one to go in."

"We'll both go," Brad decided suddenly. "It's safer that way. Let's be quick about it, and cautious."

Having made up their minds, the boys stepped

inside the hallway, closing the door behind them. The silence of the empty building was disturbing. Into their thoughts came a recollection that upon their last visit here, a door had been mysteriously locked.

Dan could feel his heart pounding against his ribs. He was scared, and unashamed of it.

Although it was still daylight, the musty church interior already was shrouded in shadow. Every cracked marble pillar stood out in the dim light as a fearful sentinel.

Dan nervously tested the door through which they had entered to make certain that it had not locked behind them.

Satisfied that the exit remained free, he then followed Brad deeper into the church.

A-tiptoe, the pair moved toward the iron stairway leading up to the belfry. The treads, they noted, were remarkably free of dust, though it lay heavy elsewhere. Cobwebs festooned other ironwork in the corridor.

Dan grasped the railing and began the steep ascent. His chest felt constricted. His breath became short, and he knew it wasn't from exertion.

The Stranger

Mid-way up to the tower, the boy halted to listen. Brad, pressing close behind, also became alert.

Neither had heard any disturbing sound. Yet they both sensed that they would run into something once they turned the next curve in the stairway.

Dan waited as long as he dared, and then crept on. Another step. Two, three, four.

Nearing the top now, he could feel a rush of cool air on his face.

Suddenly, Dan was brought up short. Above him, in the belfry, he had heard a scraping sound, as if a heavy object had been pulled across the floor.

Brad too stiffened. Afraid even to whisper, the boys huddled together, listening. From time to time they could hear slight movements in the belfry. Once they thought someone gave a deep sigh.

Finally, Dan gathered his courage and moved up another step. The bend in the stairway now lay directedly ahead. Once that point was passed, they would have a clear view of the belfry.

With Brad at his elbow, Dan negotiated the last few feet. Stunned by what he saw, he gripped the iron railing with both hands.

The great bell hung in the turret, its dark clapper

motionless. Beyond the hollow metallic vessel, almost at the edge of its flaring mouth, was a bed of blankets!

As Dan's gaze fixed upon the bedding, he beheld the figure of a drowsing man. The fellow stirred sleepily, yawned and sat up.

It was then that both Cubs saw his face clearly. The occupant of the belfry was none other than the poorly dressed stranger who had paid such marked attention to Chub at the basketball game!

CHAPTER 17

A WITNESS

THE gaunt looking man in the belfry seemed unaware of the Cubs' presence on the iron stairway.

Wrapped in heavy blankets, he sat with his back to the rim of the big bell. His feet rested comfortably on a stone ledge of the tower. He gazed lazily into space, absorbed by his own reverie.

As Dan and Brad huddled together, watching, the man presently shifted his position. His shoulder brushed against the bell, causing the clapper to swing.

"Drat it!" the man exclaimed impatiently. He seized the striker to prevent it from sounding. Having steadied the bell, he again settled down into his blankets.

The mystery surrounding the old church now had been partially solved. Dan and Brad could not guess the stranger's identity, but they were fairly certain he had been living in the belfry for days, perhaps weeks.

No imagination was required to explain the previous strange tapping of the bell and Pat's terror on Halloween night. The Bay Shore boys likely had seen this man in the belfry and had mistaken him for a ghost!

Dan's lips cracked into a grin at recollection of how Pat and his cronies had fled from the building. It really had been funny!

A bat came whirring down the well of the stairway, swooping close to the boys. Dan nearly lost his grasp on the spiral railing.

Involuntarily, he uttered a choked cry as he cringed back. Slight as was the sound, it reached the ears of the man in the belfry above.

Throwing off his blankets, he leaped to his feet.

"Who's there?" he demanded, peering down.

The daylight above seemed to have blinded him, for he did not immediately see the two boys crouching in the semi-darkness. But they could not escape detection.

"Come up out of there!" he ordered, as he made out their shadowy forms. "A couple of kids, eh?"

A Witness

Brad and Dan were nervous as they faced the stranger. The wind had blown his dark hair and he was unshaven. His eyes, however, had a friendly twinkle which slightly reassured them. They were relieved too, to note that he did not appear to be armed.

"Well, well! A couple of curious Cubs," the man said cheerfully. "So you've finally caught me?"

Already Dan and Brad had lost their fear of the stranger. He was a man of early middle age, well-built and deeply tanned from having lived an outdoor life. Why, they wondered, had he chosen the church belfry for his home?

"You've been living here a long while, haven't you?" Dan asked.

"I've been sleeping here off and on about three weeks " the stranger shrugged. "This place, I'm telling you, isn't very cozy now that the nights are so cold."

"Couldn't you have slept in the church, instead of in this bird roost?" Brad asked.

"Oh, some nights I do." The stranger had gathered up his army blankets and was folding them neatly. "I stay up here because I like the cool, clean air. I can sleep anywhere. Learned it in the army. Up here I don't have to keep an eye out all the time for that pest, Terry the Terrible."

"The church caretaker?" Dan asked, smiling at the nickname.

"Sure, he's always checking up, but never did tumble to the fact that he had a non-paying renter in his building."

"Who are you anyhow?" Dan asked bluntly. "Didn't we see you the other night at the basketball game?"

"I was there, son."

"You didn't tell us your name," Dan reminded him.

"Didn't I?" The man smiled as he ran a hand over his stubbly two-day-old beard. "Would you take me for a tramp?"

"Not exactly." Dan scarcely knew how to classify the stranger. He spoke excellent English and had certain refinements that one usually did not associate with a tramp. Yet obviously, the fellow was without funds or he wouldn't be living in the belfry.

"You must excuse my appearance," the man said. "I haven't had a chance to get to my barber yet today."

A Witness

Picking up a knapsack from the stone floor, he began to take out toilet articles—a razor, a mirror and shaving cream.

"You know you have no right to be living here," Brad burst out. "How did you get in, anyhow? Through the coal chute?"

"I did the first time. After that, I used the door."

"But this church was supposed to be locked. Terry checks on the place, or at least he's supposed to."

"The caretaker's a nice old codger, but not very alert. If he had been, he'd never have left a key lying around."

"You found it?" Brad questioned.

"It may not have been his," the stranger admitted. "I came upon it the day I holed in here. Found it lying on a window sill, and discovered it unlocked one of the doors. So I've used it ever since. Convenient."

"Terry probably was afraid to admit to the trustees that he had lost one of his keys!" Dan exclaimed. "Say, he could have cleared up a lot of things for our Den, if he'd acted right!"

No longer uneasy in the stranger's presence, the two boys now plied him with eager questions. Did he live in the belfry because he had no money? How long had he been in Webster City?

"Don't fire 'em at me so fast," the man chuckled. "I haven't been out of the army very long. I have a little money, but I'm trying to make it last until I get a certain job I'm after. Besides, I have another little matter here in Webster City—"

"Mr. Hatfield probably could help you find work," Brad offered. "He's our Cub leader."

"I'll find work all right, son. Fact is, I don't plan on staying in this town very long. Not unless—"

"Unless what?" Brad caught him up.

"Well, it depends on a certain matter. My own private affairs." Deliberately, the man changed the subject. "Tell me about the Cubs," he requested. "Do you like the organization."

"It's the best in the world," Dan said proudly.

"Don't you have a boy in your den by the name of Chub?"

"Sure," Dan agreed. "He's new. You must know him. I saw you talking to him the other night at the basketball game."

"He's a lot like my own son. I had a boy once."

"I see," Dan murmured. He remained silent, reflecting that in appearance Chub might have been

A Witness

related to this stranger. Although the color of their hair and eyes was different, the contour of their faces was much the same. A coincidence, of course. But why was this man so interested in Chub?

"I don't mind telling you about myself," the man said after a long hesitation. "First of all, I have no criminal record. I've stolen nothing and broken no law, except that I've trespassed on this property."

"You could be arrested for that," Brad reminded him.

"I know," the man admitted. "I figured that sooner or later I'd be caught here. I'll move out today. I'd hoped to stay a little longer—but never mind."

"You should tell us your name."

"I should," the man agreed. "Just call me Mr. Smith. When the right time comes, you'll learn my true name."

Brad and Dan were becoming more confused each moment. They liked the friendly stranger, but could not understand why he acted so mysteriously. If he had no criminal record, why should he hesitate to reveal his name?

"What happened Halloween night?" Dan asked curiously. "You must have played ghost."

Mr. Smith laughed aloud at the recollection. "I heard those boys sneaking up the stairway," he revealed. "I waited until they were nearly in the belfry. Then I popped out with a blanket over my face. I made moaning sounds and wild gestures. Those kids bolted out of here like a streak of lightning."

"From time to time, we've heard the bell tap," Dan went on. "Were you responsible?"

"Afraid I'll have to plead guilty. Once when the kids were here, I hit the bell by accident. The other times I tapped it on purpose. I didn't want to scare the kids too much—only wanted to keep them from playing around here."

Brad had been gazing thoughtfully at the stranger, thinking hard. If the man had lived in the belfry for three weeks, he must have observed a great many persons come and go. No wonder he seemed personally acquainted with the members of Den 2!

"Dan and I came here for a purpose today," he suddenly disclosed. "You may have heard the talk in Webster City about the Cubs causing trouble."

"I did pick up a few rumors."

A Witness

"We've been accused of doing a lot of damage here," Brad went on. "It's not true."

"I know that to be a fact."

"You do?" Brad, in his eagerness, grasped the stranger's arm. "Could you help us? That is, what I'm trying to ask—did you see anything that would help us? Do you know who really did the damage?"

"I do," the man returned. "I saw the Cubs come here that first day with their basketball. You kids smashed a window."

"That was all the damage we did though," Dan declared. "We were accused of doing a great deal more."

"The Cub honor is at stake," Brad added. "We'll do anything to prove our innocence! We think we know who did the damage, but we have no proof."

The stranger gazed down into the tense, worried faces of the Cubs. His smile was reassuring.

"I have a soft spot in my heart for the Cubs," he said. "I want to help the organization."

"Can you?" pleaded Dan. "Do you know the boys who damaged this place?"

"A gang showed up here about a half hour after the Cubs broke that window. They went through the place and really wrecked it. I saw their faces quite clearly. The ring leader, in particular, I could identify."

"Pat Oswald?"

"I don't know his name. He's captain of the Purple Five basketball team."

"That's Pat!" Dan cried. He was so excited he no longer could control his voice. "Oh, Mr. Smith, you must come with us right away to see the church trustees! If only we can make them believe the truth, the Cubs' name will be cleared!"

CHAPTER 18

A JOLT FOR PAT

DAN and Brad both were excited as the realization came to them that at last they had a means of establishing the innocence of the Cubs!

Until now, though they had been morally certain that Pat Oswald and his gang were the real culprits, they had known of no way to prove it.

But a witness miraculously had appeared! The mysterious "Mr. Smith" could, if he chose, speak the words which would clear Den 2. Would he agree to tell what he knew and had seen from the belfry?

"Will you come with us?" Dan repeated his plea. "Please, will you help the Cubs?"

"I'd like to, son," the man replied.

"Then come with us now," Brad urged. "We'll take you directly to the church trustees."

"Let's not be too hasty," Mr. Smith said. "If I tell what I know, I'll have to explain how I happened to be roosting here. That could be awkward."

"You want to help the Cubs, don't you?" Dan pleaded. "Isn't it only right that the truth should be known?"

"The truth will come out," Mr. Smith promised the boys. "It's a matter of timing though. I have to think of my own interests. I'm here in Webster City for a special purpose. If I should tell now that I've been living in this belfry—well, it might jeopardize everything I'm after."

"Then you won't go with us to the trustees?" Brad asked, bitterly disappointed.

"Let's not put it that way, son. I want to help. I will too. I'm pretty sure I can identify the boys who damaged this church. The point is, I'd like to postpone the dramatic announcement for a day or two. Wouldn't that be okay?"

"I suppose so," Brad admitted reluctantly.

"I'm getting out of this place right away," the stranger continued. "As soon as I can pick up mail at the Post Office, I'll see a certain party. Then, it may be I'll be in a position to help you. Or there may be a few days delay."

Brad and Dan could not make up their minds that they were not being "stalled." Mr. Smith seemed

A Jolt For Pat

sincere, yet how could they be sure he merely was not trying to fool them. Once they parted from him, they might never see him again.

"How will we know where to find you?" Dan asked dubiously. "We can't come back here or we'll be accused of breaking in."

"I can't stay here any longer either," the stranger declared. "Tell you what! When is your next basketball game?"

"Friday night," Brad informed him.

"I'll see you at the church gymnasium then. That will give me a few days to wind up my business here. Also, I'll be on hand to identify that boy you call Pat."

"Say, that might work out all right!" Dan exclaimed. "But how do we know you'll keep your promise?"

"You'll have to accept my word."

Brad and Dan knew that they had no choice. They could not force the stranger to accompany them to see the church trustees. If they reported the man to police, undoubtedly he would disappear before they could return to his hide-out.

"I'll not fail you," the man promised, smiling as if he had read their thoughts. "Just one favor. You're to tell no one that you have seen me here."

"Not even our Cub leader?" Dan asked.

"No one."

The two boys hesitated, reluctant to give such a binding promise.

"I'll agree to come to the game Friday night," Mr. Smith went on, "but only upon condition that you keep my secret until then. How about it?"

"I guess so," Brad said unwillingly. Dan too nodded his head.

"Cub's honor?"

"Cub's honor," Dan repeated. "We won't tell anyone about seeing you here."

"I know I can trust you boys," the stranger said. He had gathered up a few belongings, and was stuffing them into a bag. "Don't look so bewildered. Everything will be explained in good time."

"There's one thing I'd like to know right now," Brad said.

"Shoot!"

"Well, maybe you can clear up the mystery of how the ice cream freezers were delivered to the Cubs. Did you see Pat Oswald and his bunch take them from the basement here?"

Mr. Smith busied himself polishing his scuffed

A Jolt For Pat

shoes with an old rag. He kept smiling to himself, apparently enjoying his own secret.

"You know all about those freezers!" Brad accused.

"Tell us how they happened to be delivered to us!" Dan requested.

"Well, it was like this," Mr. Smith said. "I overheard the Cubs talking about needing a couple of freezers. Maybe I shouldn't have done it, but I dug 'em out of the basement here, and left them at the church."

"You certainly put us in a spot," Brad informed him. "We had a swell time making the ice cream, but Terry Treuhaft came looking for those freezers. He would have made a fearful fuss, only as it happened, we didn't have 'em."

"Someone—we suspect Pat and his bunch—had swiped them," Dan explained, grinning at the recollection.

Now that the incident was half-way forgotten, his resentment at Pat gradually was fading.

"I shouldn't have done it," Mr. Smith admitted. "But no one was using those freezers. The Cubs needed 'em. So I thought I'd do them a friendly turn."

"You're certainly all for the Cubs," Dan said, studying the stranger curiously. "Is it because of Chub?"

"Well, I took a shine to the youngster."

Mr. Smith had finished picking up his toilet articles. Now that his hair was combed, his clothing brushed, he looked entirely presentable.

"You know," Dan said abruptly, "you look a lot like Chub. Same eyes—hair."

"Say, that's right!" agreed Brad, startled by Dan's observation. "Maybe you're a relative!"

"Maybe I am," the man admitted. "Maybe I'm a close relative."

"Not his father?" Dan guessed.

"Yes, his father," the stranger repeated, almost defiantly. "Anything wrong with it? You think he'd be ashamed if he knew the truth?"

"Why, no," Dan stammered. "Why should he be ashamed of you?"

"Because I've neglected him all these years," the man burst out. "Because I'm living in this belfry instead of in a decent house or hotel, the way other folks do. Because I have no job! Because if folks knew I was Chub's father they'd say I was no good."

A Jolt For Pat

"Not if it weren't true," Dan answered quietly. "Chub's terribly lonesome. He needs a Dad."

"One that he could be proud of," the man answered in a bitter voice. "It's better that I go away and never tell him the truth!"

"Would that be fair to Chub?" Brad asked.

"It might be the kindest thing I could do. He has a good home here. I've checked into that."

"Chub has a good home," Dan agreed, "but he isn't happy. He's always mooning around, not talking much, but sort of wrapped in his own thoughts. He needs a Dad."

"Your name isn't Smith," Brad took up the discussion. "Is it Weldon, the same as Chub's?"

"That's right. He doesn't know who I am though."

Chub's father remained silent for some minutes. Then, apparently having made up his mind to tell the Cubs everything about himself, he said:

"Things are coming to a head fast. I expect to pull out of Webster City in a few days at the latest. I haven't decided yet whether or not to tell Chub that I'm his father. Can I depend upon you boys to keep the secret—at least for the time being?"

"Of course," Brad said at once.

"We wouldn't tell Chub unless you gave us permission," Dan added. "That wouldn't be square."

"My real name is Bruce Weldon," the man disclosed. "I'll not go too much into the past, except to say that some years ago through no fault of my own, I lost touch with Chub."

"How?" Brad inquired.

"Well, in a divorce proceeding, his custody was awarded to my wife. Chub was only a baby then and needed a mother to look after him. I sent money regularly for his care. That is, I did until I was wounded while serving at the front. For months, I lay in a hospital, but through a mix-up of records, I was reported missing in action."

"Then what happened?" Dan asked, deeply interested in the story.

"Eventually, I recovered and started checking up. I learned then that my wife had died, and that Chub had been placed in the home of one of her friends.

"When I inquired there, I discovered that the arrangement hadn't worked out well, and that he had been shifted elsewhere. To make a long story short, it took me nearly six months to trace Chub to Webster City. Meanwhile, I'd spent most of my

A Jolt For Pat

money, and I couldn't take a job, because I didn't want to settle down until I found Chub."

"Now that you've found him, why not tell him who you are?" Brad suggested. "Wouldn't that straighten everything?"

"It's not that simple," Mr. Weldon replied. "I've made a contact with Juvenile Court authorities, but the director isn't satisfied it would be for Chub's best interests to let me have him again. You see, it hinges on my ability to support him. I know I can get a good job and keep it too, but the court demands proof."

"Have you talked to Mr. Greene?" Dan questioned. "He's real nice and might help you."

"I know Mr. Greene very well."

"I guess he knows about Chub too," Dan said, recalling the visit of the Cubs to Juvenile Court. "Gee, it was sort of funny! I actually thought Chub might have been in trouble with the court, because everyone there seemed to be acquainted with him. It was only because they were looking out for his rights."

"Chub never was in trouble in his life," Mr. Weldon said proudly. "He's a mighty good youngster, bright in school too. Mr. Greene assured me of that.

His only problem is that he isn't very happy."

"Being a Cub though, has helped," Brad said. "He's more sure of himself, and he hardly ever stutters any more unless he's excited."

Mr. Weldon nodded and made the boys a promise. "I'll always stick up for the Den 2 boys. You know why? They were kind to Chub and didn't tease him. Now about cleaning up those accusations against the Cubs. Shall we do it on the night of the basketball game?"

"That would be the best time," Brad agreed. "How will we arrange it?"

"Leave that to me," said Mr. Weldon confidently. "Just have Mr. Greene attend the game, and if possible the trustees of this church."

"I'll get 'em there, if I have to give them free tickets to the game!" Dan chortled. "Wow! What a sockaroo Pat Oswald has in store! Even if he and his gang win that Friday game, they're going to get the jolt of their lives!"

CHAPTER 19

CUB HONOR

THE church gymnasium was jammed with spectators. Every seat had been taken ten minutes in advance of the scheduled game between the Cubs and the Purple Five. Now, crouched in a tight little knot at one end of the floor, the Den 2 boys were awaiting the starting signal.

Dan's gaze roved over the audience. In the front row not far from where his own parents sat, he sighted both Mr. Maxwell and Mr. Brennan.

He heaved a sigh of relief. Actually, he hadn't dared hope that the church trustees would attend the game, even though he had mailed them tickets.

Dan's searching eyes traveled on through row upon row of spectators. Toward the back of the gymnasium, he saw Mr. Greene, the Juvenile Court director, and another court official he did not know by name.

"Everyone's here," he whispered jubilantly.

"Everyone except Mr. Weldon," Brad replied and

his voice was tense with worry. "What if he doesn't show up?"

"He promised, didn't he?"

"Sure, but we haven't seen him since that day in the belfry. Maybe he's skipped town. Tell you the truth, Dan, I'm jittery. If he doesn't come to identify Pat, what'll we do?"

"He'll come," Dan said.

Though he spoke confidently, he too shared the older boy's uneasiness. Twice since the two had seen Mr. Weldon in the church belfry, they had returned to seek him. They had found only a locked, and apparently deserted church. The stranger who had claimed to be Chub's father, obviously had moved out immediately after his meeting with them. Had he left Webster City? They had no way of knowing, but they had not once seen him on the street.

As for the game itself, feeling was running high. The greater percentage of rooters seemed to favor the Cubs, but one section of the gymnasium was jammed with friends of Pat and the Bay Shore boys. Dan wondered how they would take a loss of the game, or a disclosure that the Purple Five team was wanted in Juvenile Court.

Cub Honor

"I feel sort of sorry for Pat," he remarked privately to Dan. "The guy doesn't have a suspicion of what's going to happen to him."

"Assuming that Mr. Weldon shows up."

"Pat isn't such a bad sort when you get to know him," Dan went on. "He's a show off, of course, and full of mischief. He's quieted down a lot though lately."

"Conscience hurting you, Dan?"

"No such thing! If Pat and his bunch wrecked that old Christian Church, then it's only right that they take their medicine. I'm not forgetting that they let the blame fall on the Cubs."

Brad glanced nervously at the wall clock. "Three more minutes until game time," he said. "I only hope the Cubs win! It's terribly important, because if Pat's team wins, and then everything breaks wide open, they may accuse us of putting the finger on 'em to get even."

Not only Dan and Brad, but all of the Cubs were exceedingly nervous. This third game in the series was the deciding one. The Den 2 boys did not so much mind losing, but they hoped that they would play their best.

The line-up however, was discouraging. Chips,

although out of quarantine, had not been permitted to play. He sat in the audience, beside Mr. Hatfield, looking pale and dejected.

Brad would play center, as always. Red and Midge were assigned as guards, while Dan and Chub were forwards. That left only Fred as substitute, which meant that the Cubs would have to take care not to be put out on personal fouls.

"If we only had Chips in the game, we'd have a chance at least," Brad confided to his friend. "But Chub—"

"He's improved a lot this last week," Dan said loyally. "I've been helping him every night after school, teaching him a few tricks. He's pepped up a great deal."

"I've noticed that," Brad admitted, turning to look at the younger boy, who even now was practicing baskets. "Do you suppose he could know—"

"About his father? I've wondered the same thing, Brad. He hasn't dropped a word, but the last couple of days he's seemed on fire. He's been so jolly and so full of pep. I just hope he's that way tonight."

The sounding of a whistle warned the Cubs that it was game time. They huddled together for a

Cub Honor

last-minute conference, then trotted out to their places on the floor.

"Come on, Cubs!" yelled the Den 2 rooters.

"Get in there, Pat!" shouted the Purple Five supporters. "Show 'em your stuff!"

The game started fast. The Purple Five had elected to take the south basket in the first half.

As the Cubs fully expected, the Purple Five center was inches taller than Brad. He out jumped his opponent, and easily tapped the ball to Pat in the first second of play.

Red though, was on his toes. He guarded Pat so closely that he could not pass or shoot for the basket. The referee tossed the ball between them. Red out jumped his opponent, and sent the ball bouncing toward Chub.

The boy missed it, but recovered. He hesitated, uncertain what to do.

"Shoot it to Dan!" shouted Chips from the sidelines.

Chub heard and hurled the ball. The shot was wild, but Dan made a leap into the air and caught it. The crowd roared with delight.

"Shoot! Shoot!" screamed the Den 2 rooters.

The ball went smoothly from Dan's hands. It

made a high loop and with scarcely a sound, dropped through the north basket.

The Cubs had scored two points in the first three minutes of play!

Thrilled by their success, the Cubs tried harder than ever for victory. However, the Purple Five were not to be caught napping a second time. Pat and his teammates began to play less cautiously, always watching for a chance to shatter the defense of the Cubs.

The Den 2 plays were working perfectly until the ball reached Chub. Repeatedly, Brad or Midge fed him the ball, only to have him muff the shot. Whenever possible, they passed to Dan, but both Purple Five guards concentrated on him.

"They watch me like a hawk," Dan complained as the two teams rested at the end of the first quarter. "If I could just get a free shot at that basket once in a while!"

The score stood 2 to 6 in favor of the Purple Five. The Cubs truly were worried. Unless they dug in fast, they'd lose the game.

Chub touched Dan on the arm. "Why don't you put Fred in instead of me?" he asked. "I—I try, but I can't seem to find the basket."

Cub Honor

Dan slapped him on the back. "You're doing fine," he said. "Quit worrying and just think about the game."

"I wanted to do well tonight 'specially," Chub said. "There's someone here watching me—"

Dan had forgotten entirely about Chub's father. Now he saw the other boy turn and glance directly at a man who stood at the end of the gymnasium with a group of spectators who had arrived too late to obtain seats.

So Mr. Weldon had kept his promise! Dan felt a great load drop from his shoulders. What a surprise Pat would get, when the game finally ended!

Dan saw Chub wave to his father, and noted the happy light in the boy's eyes.

"He knows the truth," Dan instantly decided. "Someone has told him. That's why he's trying so hard tonight. He wants to make good for his father."

Just then Mr. Hatfield came across the floor to speak to Dan. Drawing him aside, he asked his opinion about keeping Chub in the game.

"Fred doesn't particularly want to play," the Cub leader said. "Chub has missed a good many chances to score though. If you take him out—"

"No, try him awhile longer," Dan replied quickly.

195

"Chub is playing better tonight than he ever did before. Let him stay in. After all, winning isn't everything."

"I'm glad to hear you say that, Dan," Mr. Hatfield answered. "This has been a good clean game so far, and that's what counts. Excellent sportsmanship on both sides."

The game went on, and for a while the Cubs played with renewed energy. Chub managed a basket and the fans cheered madly.

But the next minute, Pat captured the ball. Before Red could stop him, he dribbled down the floor, cut in under the basket and scored.

Dan was annoyed at himself. He was playing well but the Purple Five guards wouldn't give him a chance. Time and again they deserted Chub entirely to concentrate their attention on him.

Even so, he twice broke through and made spectacular shots. At the end of the half the score stood 8 to 6, with the Purple Five leading by only one basket.

"We may take 'em yet," Dan said grimly as he rested with his teammates. "Bear down, fellows."

Baskets were held to a minimum in the third quarter. The players all were tiring. Mr. Hatfield

Cub Honor

took Chub out of the game for awhile, substituting Fred. When the Purple Five ran up two baskets in quick succession, he called Fred to the bench and let Chub go in again.

The Cubs truly were discouraged. With the score at 12 to 6 it seemed to them they were sunk.

"Come on, Cubs!" the rooters pleaded. "The old fight."

Dan gritted his teeth and tried harder than ever. He leaped for a high one, and fastening upon the ball, ran full tilt into a Purple Five guard. He pivoted, faked a pass to Chub, and dropped the ball through the basket.

After that, playing as if inspired, he scored again. Once he tangled briefly with a Purple Five guard, and the referee called a personal foul on both players. The Purple Five player missed the free throw, while the Cubs again scored.

With less than a minute to play, the tally now was: 12 to 11 in favor of the Purple Five.

"One basket would do it," Dan thought desperately. "If we don't snag it, we'll lose by a single point."

How much time was left? A minute at best. Perhaps only seconds. Assured of victory, Pat and his teammates were playing a delaying game. Without trying to make another basket, they merely sought to prevent a Cub from getting his hands on the ball.

It seemed to the frantic Cubs that they couldn't shatter the tight defense. Pat dribbled the ball lazily, passing it to a player in the middle of the floor.

"Get in there! Break it up!" Chips and Fred yelled from the sidelines. "Thirty second to play!"

Thirty seconds! Holy Mackerel, the game was the same as over! Dan breathed heavily. He was winded, and sick with the fear of defeat.

Only one basket was needed—only one.

Then Dan saw his chance. Still employing "keep it away" tactics, Pat lazily passed the ball to the forward who guarded Chub. The player missed the catch and the ball rolled free.

Like a flash, Dan darted in and seized it.

"Stop him!" Pat yelled.

Both guards were on Dan in an instant. They boxed him in, making it impossible for him to have an unobstructed shot for the basket.

Dan knew that he never could score. True, he could make a wild shot, but it never would find its mark.

Chub, however, stood unguarded a little beyond the center of the floor.

Dan passed the ball to him. Chub caught it squarely, then hesitated.

Only a few seconds now remained. Dan saw the time keeper starting to raise his hand in signal. Another instant and the game would be over.

"Shoot," he yelled. "Shoot, Chub!"

The younger Cub still seemed to hesitate. For a dreadful moment, Dan thought that he intended to try to pass the ball back.

Then Chub took careful aim and attempted the longest basket of his life. The ball looped high, striking the backstop.

The Cub rooters groaned, certain that Chub had missed. But the ball came down, striking the rim of the basket.

There it teetered while the spectators as one, held their breath. Then it dropped through the netting.

At the same moment, the game came to an end. The score read: 13 to 12 in favor of the Cubs.

"Golly, did I really make that basket?" Chub demanded, dumbfounded.

Dan and the other Cubs rushed over to clap him on the back.

"You were swell!" Brad assured him. "You too, Dan," he added warmly. "If you'd tried to grandstand that last shot yourself, the Cubs would have lost. It was teamwork that saved the game!"

Chub's eyes sparkled with delight. "Know something?" he confessed. "When I made that last shot, I-I closed my eyes. I was scared I'd miss because I always do on the long shots. So I just closed my eyes and said a little prayer."

"No matter how you did it, the Cubs won!" Dan chuckled. "I wonder how Pat and his boys will take it?"

The Purple Five, discouraged by defeat, had gathered in a little knot across the room. Pat could be seen talking to the group very earnestly, but what he might be saying the Cubs could not guess.

Chub, greatly excited, was unable to contain his enthusiasm.

"T-This was the biggest thrill of my life," he declared. "Did I really do all right?"

"Swell," Red assured him patiently.

"I'm glad," Chub sighed. "Being a Cub means so much to me. But I've never been able to carry my end."

Cub Honor

"You did tonight," Dan said. "You're a credit to the team and to Den 2."

"I'll remember that always," Chub replied soberly. He slipped away then into the crowd. Dan saw him join his father and they both went off together.

The crowd already was filing out of the gymnasium. Brad came hurrying over to speak to Dan.

"Say, we must work fast!" he announced breathlessly. "Mr. Greene and those church trustees are leaving!"

"They can't do that until Mr. Weldon tells what he knows!" Dan exclaimed in dismay. "He's supposed to identify Pat and his bunch!"

"We're making a mess of it," Brad declared. "This was supposed to be our big moment, and what happens? Everyone pulls out!"

"You stop Mr. Greene and the trustees," Dan directed. "Take them to the clubroom. I'll fetch Mr. Weldon."

"Okay, but hurry," Brad advised.

Dan started off in search of Chub and his father. He was annoyed at himself for having let them get out of his sight. Now they seemed to have vanished completely.

As he searched, Pat Oswald sought him, diffidently offering his hand.

"The Cubs played a dandy game," he said. "You deserved to win."

"Why, thanks," Dan replied, hiding his astonishment.

He shook Pat's hand and then felt suddenly almost ashamed of himself. In another minute or two, he'd be accusing this same boy in front of Mr. Greene and the church trustees. It didnt' make sense.

"Anything wrong?" Pat asked curiously.

"Plenty." Dan spoke in cold misery. But he couldn't tell him the truth even then. This was the hour the Cubs long had awaited. If he weakened now, Den 2 might never clear its dishonored name.

"You look sort of funny," Pat said, staring hard at him. "Guess you played too hard."

Dan shook his head. "I'm looking for Chub and a man with him," he said. "Have you seen them?"

"They left the church together."

"Left the church?" Dan repeated in disbelief. "Why, Chub hadn't even changed his clothes!"

"He slipped a pair of jeans over his shorts and went that way. They must have been in an awful hurry. The man just hustled him into a taxi and off they went."

Dan stared at Pat, drinking in the words. Why, it was incredible!

"You're telling me straight?" he demanded.

"Sure." Pat grinned, and added impudently: "Cub's honor!"

Dan felt completely deflated. He knew without checking that Pat had spoken the truth. For some unknown reason, Mr. Weldon has hustled his son away from the gymnasium. Deliberately, he had welched on his promise to clear the Cubs! Now the true story might never be disclosed publicly.

"Say, you *are* sick," Pat said with concern. "Anything I can do?"

Dumbly, Dan shook his head. "You've done it already," he said. "The Cubs lost everything they valued tonight."

"I don't get it," Pat said, looking puzzled. "You won the game, didn't you?"

"What's a game? More than victory or anything else, the Cubs cherished their good name in the community."

Pat stared at Dan a moment. "What's that got to do with me?" he demanded.

"I think you know, I'd hoped that tonight the Cubs might clear themselves of the untruths that have been told about them. Now I know that chance is gone."

With dignity, Dan turned and walked away from Pat into the dressing room.

CHAPTER 20

PROOF

IN the clubroom, the Den mothers were serving hot chocolate and home baked cookies to the Cubs and their friends.

When Dan stepped into the room which buzzed with conversation, he noted at once that the Bay Shore boys had not accepted an invitation to share refreshments. This was not surprising, for in previous games Pat and his followers had left the building immediately after the contest.

As he scanned the crowd, Brad and Midge came over to speak to him.

"Have you seen Chub?" the Den Chief asked anxiously.

Before Dan could reveal what he knew, Brad went on: "Right after the game, he came to me and thanked me for being nice to him. Said the Cubs all had been swell, and he wanted me to tell them so for him. I didn't think much about it at the time. But now I'm worried."

"Chub's gone."

"Gone where, Dan?"

"I dont know. But I have a hunch he's with his father, and that we'll never see either of them again."

Dan then related his own last meeting with Chub and recounted Pat's report of seeing the two leave the church together in a taxi.

"Mr. Weldon must have decided to skip town and take Chub with him!" Brad gasped. "Gosh! Where does that leave us?"

"Just where we came in." Dan spoke dejectedly. "Without Mr. Weldon, we can't prove a thing! We're sunk!"

"I asked the church trustees and Mr. Greene up here too," Brad groaned. "They're talking to Mr. Hatfield now."

He jerked his head to indicate the chocolate table where the four men stood. Mr. Greene had accepted a cup of cocoa from one of the mothers. Mr. Maxwell and Mr. Brennan, however, had refused the refreshments.

Proof

As Brad glanced in their direction, the Cub leader motioned for the boys to join the group.

"Brad," Mr. Hatfield said, "Mr. Maxwell tells me that he and Mr. Brennan received an urgent request to come here tonight. Is it true someone told them that evidence would be produced tonight to clear the Cubs of charges against them?"

"Dan sent the tickets," Brad said. "I asked the trustees up here. Dan and I did have the evidence, but we can't produce it now."

"So?" Mr. Maxwell inquired. He began to put on his gloves. "We've wasted our time. I might have known it was another Cub trick."

"But it wasn't!" Dan burst out indignantly. "The Cubs never did damage your old church. We could tell you who did do it, but we have no proof. Anyway, you wouldn't believe us!"

Mr. Maxwell ignored Dan completely. He turned to Mr. Hatfield.

"Our attorney will file suit in the morning," he announced. "We have been very patient in trying to make a settlement with the Scout organization. Now we are tired of waiting. Good evening."

He picked up his hat and started for the door.

Mr. Brennan, obviously embarrassed by such outspoken words, hesitated and then followed.

Before the pair reached the door, it opened and in poured Pat Oswald and all the Bay Shore boys.

"Hold it!" Pat called out. "Everybody listen!"

Dan thought that the Purple Five players must have come to collect their share of the game receipts.

Therefore, he was amazed when Pat pulled a cloth bag from his jeans and shoved it at Mr. Hatfield.

"Here's the money from the first game," he said. "We don't want it."

"Why, thanks, Pat," said the Cub leader. "The Cubs can use it, I guess, as we have a lawsuit to fight."

"That's why we're here," Pat announced. The room was very still now and his voice seemed raspy. "We've talked it over, and we want to make a clean breast of everything. Then you can take us to jail."

"Go ahead, Pat," Mr. Hatfield encouraged. "What is it you want to say?"

"It wasnt the Cubs who wrecked the old church," the boy blurted out. "We did it and they got the

Proof

blame. We saw a window smashed, so we smashed another and climbed inside. We didn't mean to do any real damage—we just didn't think."

No one spoke for a moment after Pat had made his confession. Finally, Mr. Maxwell said:

"Well, this does throw a different light on the matter. But how do we know they're telling the truth?"

"We wouldn't lie," Pat retorted scornfully. "Anyhow, why would we tell you this if it weren't so? It only gets us into a peck o' trouble."

Mr. Greene, the Juvenile Court director, now moved forward to face the church trustees.

"The boy is telling the truth," he said quietly. "For weeks, our department has been making an investigation. We weren't ready to make an announcement, lacking absolute proof."

"You haven't it now, either," Mr. Maxwell snapped. "You're a personal friend of Mr. Hatfield, and that's why you're siding with the Cubs."

The disclosure that Pat and his boys were responsible for the damage had not pleased him. He knew well enough that their parents were not well-to-do and the boys themselves never would be able to pay.

A silence fell upon the room. Then Mr. Hatfield's voice rang out, clear and confident.

"We do have the proof."

His dramatic, confident statement electrified and thrilled everyone. The Cubs scarcely could believe that the wonderful words had been spoken. Why, Mr. Hatfield never so much as hinted that he had learned the truth! How had he come upon his information?

Flashing a confident smile, the Cub leader took a long, fat envelope from his pocket.

"Documentary proof," he said. "This is a letter from a man who was an eye-witness of what occurred at the the old church. Rather, it is a sworn statement which he signed in the presence of witnesses."

"Not from Chub's father?" Dan cried eagerly.

"Yes, Dan. The letter came to me late today. Mr. Weldon and his son have left Webster City."

"For good?" Red asked, sorry to hear the news.

"Oh, Chub will be back from time to time. His father had obtained an excellent job in a city about fifty miles from here. Mr. Greene, though, can tell you more about that."

The Juvenile Court director took up the report.

Proof

"Chub has been a ward of the court for some time," he informed the Cubs. "He's never been happy living in a foster home. When his real father claimed him, we were glad to reunite them. However, we had to be assured that Mr. Weldon could support his son, before sanctioning the arrangement."

"Now everything has been settled?" Brad questioned.

"Yes, we gave Mr. Weldon permission today to take his son. Chub wanted to play in the basketball game, so they waited for that."

"Why didn't he come and say goodbye?" Chips demanded, hurt.

"I can answer that," Mr. Hatfield replied. "He was afraid he'd break down if he stayed. Anyway he and his father had to catch a train. He left a note though, for the Cubs. We'll read it at a closed meeting of the organization."

"Let me see that signed document," Mr. Maxwell directed. "The one you say was signed by an eye witness to happenings at the old church."

Mr. Hatfield offered him the sheet of paper which bore a notary's seal. It was a document, the Cubs knew, which would stand up in any court.

In grim silence Mr. Maxwell read the statement. Then he handed it over to Mr. Brennan.

"I'm sure you must agree now that you have no case against the Cubs," Mr. Hatfield said.

"Maybe we haven't," Mr. Maxwell admitted reluctantly. "We'll drop our suit. But these other boys ought to be locked up!"

Mr. Greene said in an even voice: "If you insist upon preferring charges, the court will consider them. However, our investigation already has disclosed that the building often was left unlocked. Terry Treuhaft was not the most careful caretaker."

"Well, someone ought to pay for the damage!" Mr. Maxwell muttered.

"Isn't it true that the building has been sold?" Mr. Greene pursued the matter. "I was informed today that the trustees have disposed of the old church at a very high figure. I was given to understand that the structure will be demolished, the materials salvaged and another building constructed."

Mr. Maxwell drew in his breath, astonished by the Court director's knowledge. Then surprisingly, he relaxed and smiled.

"It is true, we have sold the building" he ad-

Proof

mitted. "You're right. We can afford to forgive and forget."

After that, everyone suddenly seemed in good humor. Mrs. Hatfield pressed a cup of chocolate into Mr. Maxwell's hand, while Midge's mother urged Mr. Brennan to have "just one more cookie." Soon everyone was laughing and talking together, and past events were entirely forgotten.

Pat and the other Purple Five players would have slipped away, had Dan not stopped them. They too were urged to remain for music and refreshments.

"I guess they aren't going to send me to jail after all," Pat said, sipping his hot chocolate with keen enjoyment. "It was a close call though!"

"Better be careful in the future," Dan advised.

"You bet!" Pat agreed. "We're through with all that stuff. Y'know, it only gets you into trouble. No more smashing windows or swiping things for us!"

"Such as ice cream freezers?"

"Sure, we took 'em that night of the party," Pat admitted sheepishly. "We've been ashamed of it ever since too. The Cubs were swell to us—treated us square even when we were mean to them."

"Cubs always try to do things the right way,"

Dan replied. "You know the code?"

Pat shook his head.

"'A Cub is Fair; A Cub is Happy; A Cub is Game.'"

"And above all, a Cub values his honor," added Mr. Hatfield, who had overheard the two boys talking. "Thanks to you, Pat, Den 2 again will have a good name in Webster City."

Pat cast his eyes down, still feeling ashamed.

"It must be great to be a Cub and belong to the Pack," he said at length. "It's a lot better than a gang, isn't it?"

"A great deal better, Pat."

"But Cubs wouldn't be for—for kids like me."

"Why not?" Mr. Hatfield asked quietly. "From the start, I had hoped to interest you boys in the organization. That was why I favored the basketball games."

"You mean we can join the Cubs?"

"You certainly can," Mr. Hatfield assured him. "Since you live in another part of town it wouldn't be practical to come here often. But you could have your own den. I'll help you find a leader and organize."

"You will?" Pat's freckled face lighted like a

Proof

Christmas tree. "Gee! Wait until I tell the fellows!"

The Bay Shore boys all shared Pat's desire to join the Cub organization. Eagerly they asked for detailed information. Pat especially wanted to know if they might play another series of basketball games the following season.

"Of course," Mr. Hatfield promised. "Den 2 will be glad to play your den."

"Our den!" Pat liked the sound of the word. "Say, that's something! We'll have uniforms too, won't we? And pins?"

"Everything that goes with Cubbing."

"There's just one thing more," Pat said. He cast his eyes down, and then went on quickly. "About wrecking that cardboard fort. A couple of the fellows did it and then were sorry. If we could rebuild it or anything—"

"We'll talk about that later," Mr. Hatfield said. "Just now, so that you'll feel you're really being taken into one of the finest organizations in the world, we want to introduce you to the Living Circle."

"What's that?" Pat asked suspiciously.

"We'll show you," Dan offered.

Joining with the Bay Shore boys, the Cubs formed

a circle. Each youngster faced inward, extending his left hand, palm downward, into the circle. Each Cub then grasped the thumb of the boy to his right, raising his free hand in the organization's sign.

"Are we really Cubs now?" Pat asked, his eyes gleaming.

"Not yet, but soon," Dan answered with a friendly grin. "You fellows have plenty to learn.

"The salute?" Pat chuckled. "Nothing to that. He raised his right hand, smartly paying deference to all the Cubs.

"There are even more important things, Pat."

"Don't I know?" the Bay Shore boy drawled. "Honor and honesty and loyalty to friends. It may take me a long while, but with your help, Dan, someday I'll be the fairest, squarest Cub of the lot!"

THE END